THE PORTRAIT PAINTER

Georgiana Rankin's passion has always been painting, following in the footsteps of her beloved Pa. When the opportunity to produce a family portrait of the prestigious Merryfields is offered, she takes it — hoping her past will not catch up with her. Meanwhile, Kit Merryfield, the eldest son and heir, is making his way back home after being wounded in the Peninsular War. Both he and Georgiana are in for a surprise when he arrives — for they have met before . . .

BETH JAMES

THE PORTRAIT PAINTER

Complete and Unabridged

LINFORD
Leicester

First published in Great Britain in 2016

First Linford Edition
published 2017

A catalogue record for this book is available
from the British Library.

ISBN 978–1–4448–3435–2

Published by
F. A. Thorpe (Publishing)
Anstey, Leicestershire

Set by Words & Graphics Ltd.
Anstey, Leicestershire
Printed and bound in Great Britain by
T. J. International Ltd., Padstow, Cornwall

This book is printed on acid-free paper

1

Kit Merryfield, his arm casually draped over the back of a chair, his face tilted at a three-quarter angle, stood in what was meant to be a relaxed pose and surveyed the scene in front of him. The trouble was, the scene in front of him was unutterably dull. There was a mere smidge of tall sash window in his view, permitting him only the veriest glimpse of sky and treetop, so he was unable even to stare down onto the street and watch his neighbours or their visitors — which, because his neighbours belonged to the elite and fashionable *ton*, might have proved at least a little amusing.

He scowled. He would rather be out on the town with his cronies, or up in Yorkshire with his fishing rod, than standing — under scrutiny, and decked out in his new uniform — feeling like a jackass. Actually, it wasn't the uniform he objected too. He was mighty proud of *that*. It was the boredom. It was the posing, for that was all it could be called: *posing* for an old man and his urchin son, the pair of them sizing him up with their eyes then scribbling in their sketchbooks. Later, their work would be transferred to a canvas and goodness knew what sort of a job they would make of that. Probably he'd be depicted as a beanpole with a too-large nose, a bush of dark hair, and scrawny arms and legs. Well, at least that would be no more than the truth!

He ran a finger round the inside of his collar, afterwards being careful to return his hand to its original position. Then he became aware of an itch on his nose, soon to be followed by a desire to move his leg which was beginning to signify that pins and needles would soon set in. If it weren't for his father's indeterminate health, there'd be no bearing it. But his father had insisted that he wanted a likeness of his eldest

2

son in his uniform completed before he went off to war, and the old artist chap sitting in the corner, now narrowing his eyes as he inspected Kit's gangly form, had come highly recommended, was said to be proficient and quick . . .

Quick! Kit paused on the thought and scowled some more. The first sitting had been bearable. George Rankin was friendly enough, with eyes that held a twinkle which Kit couldn't help but take to. He'd exchanged pleasantries with Kit and asked intelligent questions about his expectations for his career. The strangely mute urchin who helped him with his equipment turned out to be his son, and was of carroty complexion.

'Don't mind Georgie,' said George Senior. 'He's my son. Clever lad, but shy . . . Learning the trade, you know. Good apprentice, good eye, good colour craft.'

'Really?' said Kit, barely smothering a yawn, and looking down his nose at the ferrety-faced youth in his too-big clothes and cloth cap.

'He won't bother you. Just sits in the corner and watches and draws.'

And that was what he did; only, by this second session, slowly but surely, Kit had become aware that the cold appraising gaze emanating from Georgie's corner was unsettling. Being stared at to that degree was, damn it, nothing short of unnerving.

Sometimes, Kit allowed his eyes to slide from his meagre view of the London sky outside, and settle for a fleeting moment on the young lad's inscrutable gaze. He'd then feel a second's satisfaction as the cool grey glance slipped away from direct contact, only to alight a little later on Kit's shoulders, or his arm — or, worse still, his legs, which Kit was well aware could only be described as *skinny*.

'Army will make a man of you, Christopher,' his father had told him with pride. 'You'll soon fill out. Taste of battle, do you the world of good.' Then his expression had softened. 'But don't take unnecessary risks ... Besides being damned fond of you, you're all I have of your mother,' he'd added gruffly. And Kit had coloured up because the name *Arabella* hung in the air between them as tangibly as though it had been spoken.

So now here he was, having his portrait painted, disliking every minute of it, and blushing like a girl at the mere thought of Arabella's name. Arabella, his father's second wife, which made her his stepmother — and he'd do well to remember it. Beautiful Arabella. Kit clenched his fists. How he hated her!

'Getting tired?' George Senior shifted in his chair. 'The preliminary sketches are taking shape now. We should be able to start on the canvas tomorrow. After that, a few sessions for colour work, and then the remainder of the job can be done in the studio without your help.'

Instantly, Kit snapped himself back into young-aristocrat-cum-first-rate-officer, going-off-to-fight-England's-archenemy-old-Boney, mode.

'I'm good enough,' he replied, straightening his tense shoulders and moving his numb leg. 'Don't stop on my account.'

George's eyes twinkled at him. 'In that case, sir, I'll just step outside for a moment, stretch my legs. They're not so young as yours, and we've been working near a couple of hours.'

Kit felt his face flush. Of course; how could he have been so unthinking? The poor man was hinting for a halt in the proceedings; in order to answer a call of nature, perhaps. Anyway, the emptiness of his own stomach told him it was way past time for luncheon.

Standing now, George flexed his shoulders and rubbed at his eyes — which, despite their twinkle, looked slightly inflamed.

'I ordered a tray to be sent up,' said Kit, stretching his own body, which felt stiff with tedium rather than fatigue. 'I'd have thought it would be here by now.'

'Thank you, sir,' George twinkled

again. 'That would be most welcome.' He nodded towards the corner. 'Won't be long, Georgie.'

The urchin in the corner stirred, but remained seated. 'Alright, Pa,' he muttered in an oddly husky voice. His eyes followed his father until the door closed, then he hunched back over his sketchbook.

There was a clatter of hooves on the road outside, and Kit turned his attention back to the window. Ah, a carriage had drawn up outside the residence next door. He moved to the window and craned his neck a little, hoping for a peek at the young lady of the house — who, besides possessing the bluest eyes Kit had ever seen, also had a neatly-turned ankle. Kit had caught glimpses of the ankle before; but, alas, this time he was not so fortunate. With a shrug of his shoulders, he turned to make his way through the room and down to the kitchens in order to chase up the tray for the artist and his son. Barely glancing in the urchin's direction, he opened the door to the corridor.

'Ah! Excellent,' he said. 'A tray has been left for you on the table outside.' He grasped it by its two brass handles and brought it into the room. 'It seems you won't starve after all.'

The pinched ferret face turned towards him; eyes twin pools of cool grey that made Kit feel slightly disconcerted. Dashed odd, he thought, for a whippersnapper of a boy to make him feel so unsettled. He'd been doing it all morning, too. Staring at every line of his face, making him conscious of every hair in his eyebrow, every twitch of his lip.

He put the tray down. 'Well then, let's see what you've been up to.' Casually, Kit leaned across to tweak the sketchbook from the boy's grasp.

There was an expulsion of breath. 'No sir!'

Kit looked up sharply. There'd been a desperate tone in the startled entreaty.

Half-amused, half-irritated, he grasped

8

the book even harder. 'It can't be that bad. I can assure you, I'm unable to draw a line that's in any way straight.'

For a brief moment there was a silent tussle. The urchin's face was flaming red.

Determined not to be bettered by an artist's brat, Kit held on firmly. For a few seconds, Georgie was half-lifted out of his seat. Kit watched as he teetered for a moment, then fell forward, crashing to his knees, his sketchbook flying in an arc to land at Kit's feet.

He stooped to pick it up.

Good God.

The work was more than proficient. Kit gazed in awe. A nose which was high-bridged and aristocratic; two slightly hooded eyes, topped by brows that he knew only too well were over-large in proportion to the rest of his nineteen-year-old face, but which the fledgling artist had used to catch a certain vulnerability. He scrutinised further until he came to the thin upper lip resting firmly on the full lower one. It was his mouth, all right — but surely he didn't actually look so sulky, so angry?

Hardly heeding the low moan emanating from Georgie's half-crouched position on the floor, Kit turned the page.

'Good God!' This time he said the words aloud. He'd revealed two full-length sketches. Kit's torso, his legs — upper thigh and calf — met his eyes. They were good, well-proportioned sketches; but Georgie, for some reason best known to himself, had chosen to dispense with the uniform and sketch Kit's spare, angular frame as naked as he'd been born. He stared at his square shoulders, his puny torso and his skinny arms. He gave a sudden grin. Not exactly a fine example of burgeoning manhood. He'd been caught good and proper.

His first instinct was to laugh; make a joke of it. Then he turned to grip the urchin's shoulder and found himself staring at close quarters into Georgie's face. It was a pinched, undernourished lad's face. Wide-apart grey eyes, freckles over the bridge of a small snub nose, but a full mouth that was trembling now with some unspoken reaction. Kit gripped the small bony shoulder more tightly as a strange emotion took him over, because suddenly he knew he wanted to do no more than take Georgie's face between his hands and kiss those full, girlish lips.

Sick with himself and angry at the boy, he pushed him away.

The boy toppled, and with a cry of anguish clutched at his cap.

'Good God,' said Kit yet again, for as the cap dropped, a cloud of red-gold curls tumbled down to frame the urchin's face.

All at once, the ferrety features were no longer ferrety. They were dainty, feminine and delicate, and the sprinkling of freckles over the small nose — which he now realized was retroussé rather than snub — merely added to its charm. At a stroke, the features had softened, and — damn it, the urchin wasn't a boy, he was undisputedly a girl!

'What the devil?' began Kit, releasing his hold before the furious urge to shake that small body until its teeth rattled could overcome him. He became aware that a small hand was on his arm.

'I'm sorry, sir . . . Please don't tell Pa you know.'

Unbidden, the thought of those nude sketches came into his mind. He shook the hand off. 'Your father should be shot,' he said, stepping back lest he lose his temper and do something he'd later regret.

The girl had been attempting to stuff the river of red-gold hair back into her cap, but now she stopped and shot him a look of — what? Almost disdain?

Disdainful of *him*? Christopher Merryfield? Kit to his friends — but clearly she would never be one of them . . . How dared she?

The look changed to one of patient resignation, which somehow annoyed him even more. 'Well,' she said in a quietly-controlled tone. 'You might like to bear in mind that my father is a great portrait painter. I'm learning his trade . . . It's not my fault I'm a girl and have to resort to this — this subterfuge.'

There was a short silence while Kit tried to put his shocked feelings in order. 'Your father has no business to encourage you in this — this deceit. Absolutely not!' Avoiding her gaze, he took a few steps towards the window. That was better. He'd put enough distance between them so he could feel he was in charge again. 'You disgust me,' he added for good measure.

'My father is going blind,' stated Georgie, in a voice which invited no sympathy. 'We only have each other. If I were a boy, I could help him more. As it is, I help the only way I can. He can see close up, but not at the middle distance'. She indicated his chair. 'From where he's sitting, your face is a blur to him. Painting is his livelihood.'

Her voice shook. 'Please, I'm begging you, don't humiliate him by telling him you know.'

Kit risked another glance in her direction, and observed — without wanting to — the slender roundness of the form beneath the boy's clothes. How could he not have noticed before?

'How old are you?'

Georgie took a breath. 'I'm nearly fifteen, but I've been apprenticed to Pa all my life . . . I *have*.' Her chin raised a notch, and a note of pride entered her voice. 'I have a natural ability, you see. Pa says it would be sacrilege to ignore it.' She paused. 'And it's not deceit. Not if it's the only way I can use my gift. What difference does it make that I'm a girl? I'm better than a boy at drawing and painting. Pa says so, and he should know.'

'But to allow you to dress in a boy's clothes . . . It's a disgrace . . . ' Words failing him, Kit turned away. 'Staring at me . . . Imagining me in a state of undress . . . ' He swung back again and looked directly at her. 'Have you no shame?'

For a moment, her eyes flickered with hurt. Then she swallowed and gave a defiant smile. 'When it comes to drawing — no,' she said. 'That's right. I suppose I have no shame. I look at light and dark, at form and tone. I don't see clothes when I'm trying to draw a body. I don't see flesh as flesh, even — merely a covering for bones, muscle and sinew. I put down lines on paper in order to complete a portrait. I can't be too nice about what's acceptable behaviour for a girl as opposed to a boy. I have a job to do. Pa will help me, guide me, criticise me. But let me assure you that at the end of it, *your* Papa will receive his money's worth. I promise you that!'

They stood silently, staring at one another, until Kit became aware of footsteps outside. The door handle rattled. Hurriedly, he turned his attention to the tray.

George Senior entered the room. 'Ah,' he said, 'I see I'm just in time. My lad would have made short work of that without me, I'm sure.'

Kit continued to stare at the tray, only now realising what a paltry repast it offered. He strode to the fireplace and grasped the bell-rope. Then he set aside the jug of small ale and two glasses, opened the door, and picked up the depleted tray: 'Excuse me just one moment,' he said.

Hardly had he pulled the door to behind him than he saw a footman approaching.

'I'm to tell you luncheon is served, sir.'

'Ah, yes,' said Kit. 'Take this tray to the kitchen and replenish its contents. This man — ' He indicated over his shoulder to the gap between the door and doorframe; where, from the corner of his eye, he could see George Senior staring in bafflement at the space where the tray had been. ' — this man and his son are artists, not beggars. You can tell them in the kitchen that I wouldn't use that piece of stale cheese in a mousetrap!'

The footman — who, Kit estimated was about the same age as himself — opened his mouth in protest.

'If there's any argument, just remind Cook who the next master of this household will be. When the tray is returned, I expect to see today's bread, fresh ham, and a decent amount of cheese.'

'Yes sir.' After a startled glance in Kit's direction, the footman went off to do as he was bid.

Young Christopher Merryfield made an expulsion of breath. At least he'd been able to vent his fury on something. He was sick of his stepmother's autocratic ways, which invariably manifested themselves against those she considered her inferiors. A part of him hoped she'd find him out and object to his overriding her orders, then he could argue with her over the size of a piece of cheese. Something he could put into words — something tangible, something acceptable. He brooded for a moment over a host of things which were *not* acceptable. Her hand on his leg, for instance; her body brushing against his when he was least expecting it; the knowing glances bestowed on him when she thought no one was looking. Ah, indeed! But fresh bread, cheese, ham . . . oh yes, he was on safe ground there.

Come to think of it, he was dashed well hungry himself.

The door behind him was still ajar. He stuck his head around it. Two pairs of astonished eyes met his.

'Your lunch should be up in a moment,' he said. 'I'll be back in less than an hour, so we can get back to work then . . . '

The artist and his son — no, daughter — stared at him some more. Then George Senior snapped to attention. 'Thank you, sir.'

'Right,' said Kit. 'Good work. Carry on.'

As he walked down the corridor, he felt the start of a smile spread across his face. He remembered the cool grey eyes appraising his body. Cheeky chit of a girl! The smile became a grin of relief, and he chuckled out loud.

For the life of him, he couldn't remember what had made him so angry this morning.

★   ★   ★

'Well done, Georgie,' George Senior peered closely at her sketchbook images of Master Christopher Merryfield's face. 'I think you've caught him. Proud and angry, but with a passionate nature smouldering beneath.'

He'd gone.

At last father and daughter were alone. The light was fading and the afternoon's drawing was completed.

Georgiana — alias Georgie, the artist's son — smiled at her father, eased her shoulders, and rubbed her right temple. For the two hours since lunch she'd been concentrating hard. Less than half the concentration had been on her sketchpad, the main part engaged in regarding Christopher Merryfield in a purely inanimate light. This afternoon she'd worked on the details of the uniform, but it had still been near-impossible to keep her eyes from occasionally wandering to his face, and wondering what he was thinking.

To no avail. Christopher Merryfield, every inch the young soldier, stood like a statue, his gaze fixed upon the small area of sky within his field of vision, and barely blinked an eye.

Georgiana told herself she was glad about that, because she needed all her wits to focus on the work in hand.

Her father was undisputedly the master of depicting textures and folds of fabrics, but he would rely on her to furnish him with the intricacies of the uniform. George Senior would know the exact point of light that would catch on the highly-polished boot; he'd place the deepened shadow of the inside sleeve at the precise level where the elbow bent; and the shade of bluish-white on the sword handle would make it shine so that it was made of steel would be in no doubt. Those touches were the extras her father was paid to produce. They made the difference between mediocrity and excellence; and for George Rankin, only excellence would do.

So Georgie had to play her part, had to concentrate all her efforts to excellence. She had a way — a trick, Pa called it — of catching a likeness with the minimal amount of strokes. Her work was loose and unpolished as yet; but with every portrait father and daughter completed, she grew steadily more accomplished . . . and was now at the stage, since George Senior's sight was fast deteriorating, of becoming indispensable.

Georgie glanced at the sketch her father was studying. He was waiting expectantly for her to comment on it. She raised her eyebrows. What had he said, now? Oh, yes: pride, anger, and passion. Well, she couldn't mention the passionate part, not without blushing; she'd have to refer to some other quality.

'Proud — yes, I would say so. The rest — well, how can I know? I only draw what I see.'

'And what do you see?'

She shrugged. 'A privileged young man. A discontented young man.'

George Rankin chuckled. 'A bored young cub. A young man lusting after action and adventure. Maybe a little full of himself, but one who still had time to notice when the refreshments provided for us lesser mortals did not come up to scratch. Not a bad boy . . . Shows some manners, some heart.' He turned the page. 'Good work, Georgie. Not much of a frame on him yet, but you've got the proportions right. Well done . . . I fancy he'll improve with age — both physically and personally. I think he might turn out to be what they term as a regular out-and-outer, like his father before him. Sad turn of events, the day his Pa fell from his horse. Very

sad. Little more than an invalid now.'
He closed the sketchbook with a snap.
'In any event, that was the best plate
that's been set before me in this
house. There's enough cheese that I've
wrapped in paper to do us for supper
later.'

Georgiana sighed. She didn't feel
quite comfortable about secreting food
away for later. It made her feel
beholden somehow, and she didn't
want to feel beholden to Christopher
Merryfield.

Well, at any rate, she wouldn't have
to see him again. Her part in the
proceedings was over — at least, until
the studio work started. Pa would come
alone tomorrow and decide on his
colour palette, easy enough to do from
a distance. He would require his model
to stand once more so that he could
block in a rough background. The chair
he was leaning against, the carpet, the
tone of the watered silk walls; and then
the rough blocking-in of his model's
frame. Some colour-matching where

the uniform was concerned, of course, but after that it would be back to the studio where father and daughter would work together, mixing pigments and committing to memory the quantities ready for next time. It would be her responsibility to ensure that the support — in this case, the best-quality canvas — was prepared with the correct amount of gum Arabic, and primed again ready for the groundwork. Between them, they'd work on background proportions and light sources; and out of the shadows, slowly but surely, a portrait would begin to emerge. It was exciting, exhilarating work which Georgiana loved with a passion. If only she had been born a boy, then she could have worked without secrecy, without shame.

'*Have you no shame?*'

Thinking now of the angry youth's exclamation, she coloured and blinked hard in order to stop tears from forming. Oh yes, she had shame. No one could have resented more the uncomfortable necessity for disguise;

the sensation of a young boy's breeches, of a rough shirt and waistcoat against her skin. Lately, too, the constant hunching over to conceal the blossoming of a young girl's body had made her shoulders ache. And the cap that was intended to keep her hair under control was becoming more and more difficult to manage. More than once she'd had to dodge and duck as some well-meaning client had made to give her a playful cuff around the head. She wished the dreadful subterfuge could be over, but just how that could ever be was beyond her comprehension.

Packing up the tools of their trade, she sighed again.

'Tired, Georgie? It's been a long session. You'll be glad to get out of that gear, no doubt . . . ' He looked round at the easel and folding stools stacked neatly to one side, along with the wooden box full of pencils and chalks and roughly-put-together colour guides consisting of daubs of paint for consideration and matching. 'We can be on our way now. Back to the studio and out of those clothes, and I'll have my clever, resourceful Georgiana back. What would I do without you, eh?'

'You'd manage very well,' she answered automatically, even though both of them knew it wasn't true.

From now until the end of the summer, George Rankin's diary was full. Most of his commissions were for portraits: two more of young men going to war, and several of successful tradesmen and their wives. There were also some of newly-built mansions, which George always quoted more for because, although once upon a time these were his bread and butter, the recent deterioration of his eyesight now made it a trying exercise. Translating a stately home, newly-built for a member of the *nouveau riche*, onto canvas was as uninspiring to Georgiana as it was difficult. As she readily admitted, the perspective of buildings was not as yet her forte. That it was also nowhere near as exciting as watching someone's glance or smile come to life beneath her fingers was something she seldom mentioned; and, because she recognised the necessity of expanding on her natural talents, she persevered.

But the folk of the new upper-middle class (a term which she hated anyway) that was emerging through trade were proud of their achievements, and a Georgian-style house set in impressive grounds had to be depicted with care and attention to detail. Sometimes, when the mansion in question was unutterably dull, she would wash it with a glaze of rosy gold, no matter how bleak the weather. She'd found that this technique, another trick of the trade, seldom failed to impress the lady of the house, who usually liked to feel that apart from being symmetric and impressive in its grandeur, her home appeared warm and inviting.

On the whole, the Rankins enjoyed staying at the mansions of those who had risen through trade. They were looked after well there, and treated with respect. Georgiana had to be careful, of course. Stay in the background, mixing paints, carrying easels that were nearly half her weight; watching, listening, sketching; making notes on the number of windows, of embellishments to the front facia; forever drawing and helping her father to make a living.

But for now, she would be free — for the evening, at least. She followed her father down the back staircase, passing the po-faced butler, before stepping through a side entrance out onto the leafy, shady street with its tall town houses, homes of the rich. They turned their faces in the direction of across town, out towards their studio in a rougher district altogether, where they would work on the portrait.

Georgie would become Georgiana once again, in her plain gown, her flaming hair dressed neatly, her all-seeing eyes cast modestly down as she kept house and ostensibly helped her father in all else but his painting. Especially not in the portrait of a strong-featured, scowling young man on the verge of going to war. A young man who now shared her secret — and maybe, she admitted to herself, maybe a very small portion of her heart.

2

Four years later

'Georgiana, listen! This is an opportunity for you like no other.'

Georgiana stared across the group of school desks at the diminutive figure before her. Lucinda Hargreaves, dressed in a modest grey gown, her head a little on one side, bright eyes shining now with enthusiasm. Besides being her friend, Lucinda, as the head of a small and exclusive academy for young ladies, was also her employer.

The sense of her words penetrated Georgie's tired brain. 'Yes, it must seem so, and yet . . . ' She turned the thick vellum with its black scrawl over and over in her hands. 'You think it will harm me if I turn this commission down, but I have misgivings — strong misgivings.'

Lucinda's prim, birdlike figure moved as though to remonstrate, but she checked herself and gave a gentle smile. 'I do,' she said softly, 'I do think it will harm you. I think you will always regret not taking the chance. The Lord knows, we women don't get too many of those . . . And you're good. More than good. A portrait of Arabella Merryfield and her two daughters and little son will be shown off, make no mistake, and it will be remarked on in all the best drawing rooms. You will become fashionable and acceptable . . . Not that you have ever been *unacceptable*, of course. That was not my meaning. But, my dear . . . ' Lucinda came towards her and her hand touched Georgie's sleeve. 'You are worth more than I can pay you as a teacher here at my school. Oh, I know what you will say. You will say that you're perfectly happy, and the girls are all that is right and proper, and how much you enjoy teaching them, but . . . '

'But?' Georgiana's shapely brows rose.

'It's not enough, is it? Not for the long term. Not for you who are capable of so much more. Oh I know you've sold some drawings and accepted small commissions before, but not by someone as influential as Arabella Merryfield. And the offer has come at such a providential time, too. The Christmas break, a time when I can spare you!'

'But that's just the trouble,' objected Georgiana, waving the letter. 'Don't you see? It's a shade *too* convenient. Mr Merryfield is too frail and susceptible to cold to travel from Yorkshire to spend Christmas at the London house as planned, so what could be more convenient than that I escort Jane Merryfield from here to Yorkshire instead? I can hear the conversation now: *Oh, and by the way, remember the portrait painted of Christopher before he went off to war? That was by George Rankin. Maybe the daughter*

32

— who is, after all, an art teacher — can be persuaded to execute a flattering picture of the lady of the house plus her children. That way, my dear Mr Merryfield, for the price of Miss Rankin's travel, we have an ideal escort for our daughter Jane, and a cheap portrait to boot.'

'I'm sure you're exaggerating the case.'

'But all the way to Yorkshire?' Georgiana frowned. 'I don't have fond memories of the place. I've only been there once before, and that was a long time ago when Pa was alive and we were asked to paint — Aubrey House I think it was, and Squire Ashton and his wife who had a dreadful little dog that wouldn't stop yapping. Anyway, where was I? Oh yes, and Merryfield? I knew the name as soon as I met Jane in the schoolroom but thought it commonplace enough for her to be no relation, or maybe just a distant one. But, yes, I did go to the Merryfields' London house once with Pa. It was only the once to take the likeness and the details for the portrait, because although he could still see the colours and the shapes, Pa was struggling with his sight . . . Naturally, he did all the talking and I never set eyes on the Merryfields, only their son . . . ' Briefly reliving the moment when a pair of questioning dark eyes stared into hers, she broke off and absently put her hand to her throat. 'But it wasn't a welcoming house. Of course, I was posing as a boy and answering to 'Georgie'. It was even less acceptable then for a young girl to be a portrait painter, and in this case the subject was a man! Totally taboo!'

Georgiana's voice faded as she remembered again that terrible moment when her cap had fallen to the floor, the astonishment in the young man's eyes when her hair had tumbled down and he'd made the shocking discovery that the artist's apprentice was in fact a girl! But, to her further dismay, his astonishment had turned quickly to embarrassment, then anger at the realisation that she'd sketched his form dispensing with the distraction of garments.

A shiver went through her. He'd been furious. Thinking the game was up and they'd be sent from the house in disgrace, she'd been mortified. But no, Christopher Merryfield had done nothing. Well, better than nothing — he'd sent their meagre tray of food back to the kitchen and had a much-improved refreshment provided. Then he'd returned in the afternoon, posed for two more hours without complaint, and never once given any indication that he knew Georgie's secret.

As a form of gratitude or penance — she wasn't sure which — Georgie had worked on the portrait as she'd never worked before. Even now, she could picture the bones of the young man's face; the curve of his mouth; the jut of his nose. The exact manner of his stiff-backed stance, the tension in his arm as it lay on the chair back. Oh yes, she could remember it all too vividly, for back at the studio she'd completed the portrait almost single-handed.

And the portrait had been a success. Pa had been pleased, and Joshua Merryfield delighted with the likeness.

There had followed a period of relative productivity and profit for the father-and-daughter team, but as it became more and more difficult to keep up the subterfuge of Georgie's gender, George Senior started to refer to his son as being a sickly lad, and rarely called him by name in front of clients. A year later, they took a trip to the country, 'for Georgie's health'; and, once in Essex, started to work on a series of landscapes, all executed by Georgiana and signed *G. Rankin* by George Senior — which, as he said with a twinkle, was no more than the truth. They were about to return to London, announce the sad demise of poor sickly Georgie, and introduce Georgiana (alias Ann) as his daughter and housekeeper, who'd only recently discovered a small talent for landscapes in watercolour . . . when fate caught up with them.

As he was crossing a busy thoroughfare, George Rankin misjudged the distance of a heavy coach and horses, and was trampled underfoot.

That he died instantly was something Georgiana was later thankful for. She knew that Pa would have hated to be infirm.

At first, the shock had been paralysing; then followed the grief and the realisation that she was alone in the world. Eventually she'd returned to London, living in the cold, draughty studio which was little more than a shack. She'd filled her sketchbook with page after page of stark charcoal sketches outlining George Senior's features: his twinkly eyes, his slightly crooked nose, his generous mouth, and the chin which was fast becoming flabby. But somehow she couldn't bring herself to complete a full sketch of him. It was as though she could only bear to remember the separate parts. To see him as a whole would be just too painful a reminder of the depth of her loss.

In due course, the need to support herself had forced her to look through any uncompleted work, and set about finishing it and collecting payment. She'd gone through the process in a trance, but gradually the memories of Pa carefully guiding her fingers whilst he explained the tricks of the trade came back to her, making her feel closer to him; and the hurt became, if not less, then more bearable.

And then she had met Lucinda, who was standing before her now patiently waiting for her to speak. Knowing how much she owed her, Georgie swallowed. Surely she deserved an explanation as to why she would turn down such a golden opportunity.

But . . . Christopher Merryfield!

Her fingers tightened on the paper in her hand. 'I don't think I can do it,' she said almost to herself. 'I know I've never met the Merryfields and even if I had I feel sure they wouldn't remember me. But suppose they remember my father's apprentice was his son 'Georgie'. How could I be named Georgiana?'

'They know your name already. The letter was addressed to Miss Georgiana Rankin. They cannot possibly see anything amiss. In any event, you'll be addressed as Miss Rankin, you know that. The son Christopher is away with the army and can't get home for Christmas, as Jane is forever telling us. I can see no reason why you shouldn't go, and why this commission shouldn't lead to better things. Please reconsider before you turn it down.'

Georgie sighed, because she'd thought about little else since the letter had arrived yesterday. 'I have thought about it; over and over, and I always arrive at the same conclusion.'

Lucinda's head tipped to the side, making her look more birdlike than ever. 'Well, if you're so set against it, then there's nothing more I can say. But this is a chance I feel sure you should take. Oh, I know I said I'd say no more, but it would be for less than three weeks, wouldn't it? What could happen in that time? If the Merryfields are pleased with the portrait, it could be the making of you. Arabella Merryfield is a renowned beauty, you know. The rest of London — for I'm sure it would end up in their London house — would have to acknowledge that it's possible for a woman artist to be as good as a man.'

A small smile pulled at the corners of Georgie's lips. 'And less of a strain on the purse strings,' she said dryly.

'That could be to your advantage. Sir Joshua Reynolds, you know, started out only charging five guineas for a head and shoulders.'

Georgiana shook her head. 'Let's be realistic. Joshua Reynolds, indeed! I wish I shared your confidence. Women artists are more accepted in Europe now, I know that; and, thank goodness for me and my painting lessons, it's considered an attribute for any young lady to be tutored in the art of watercolour — but oil portraits? No, an artist who's a man will always be a first choice. Even the famously talented Angelica Kauffmann was taken by her father to the Royal Academy's life classes in boys clothes, so that she might improve her drawing! No, in general, women artists are frowned upon . . . It's the way of the world.'

'Unless you help change that way of thinking, it always will be!'

Lucinda turned and walked away from where Georgie was sitting at one of the schoolroom desks. When she reached the door, she paused and looked over her shoulder. 'Georgiana,' she said. 'When we first met, do you know what I immediately noticed about you?'

Georgie gave a rueful smile 'My red hair, perhaps?'

'No . . . It was your spirit! You were hungry, you were tired. You had very little money and no possessions other than that cubbyhole of a studio of your father's — but you had spirit, didn't you?' She laughed. 'You confided in me later that if I'd turned down your application for the post of teacher of art, literature and deportment, you'd even have entertained the notion of cutting your hair and reverting to the old masquerade of becoming a man. Becoming George Rankin and continuing his work as his son!' She paused for reflection and her smile became broader. 'I think you'd have done it, too! Although — ' She eyed Georgiana's figure for a moment. ' — whether you'd have got away with it is quite another thing . . . And the scandal it might have caused . . . My dear, I dread to think!'

For the first time since the letter had arrived, Georgie gave a wide grin. Yes, she had indeed contemplated the craziest of notions. But now, at nineteen years of age, she was more sensible. She shook her head sadly. 'That was years ago, Lucinda; I know better now than to consider so foolish an idea. It was all very well pretending to be a youth. Indeed, I finished three of Pa's portraits after his death; and, posing as his son, delivered them and took the payment — five guineas at the time for a three-quarter portrait, a worse deal than even Joshua Reynolds first had. But to call on prospective clients in order to promote business is a different proposition altogether; and to keep up the pretence all the time, nigh-on impossible. Indeed, Lucinda, you were the one who made me see the error of my ways.'

A gust of rain spattered against the window. Lucinda drew her shawl more closely round her shoulders. 'Yes, because it was imprudent. You would have been found out and, in the ensuing scandal, the quality of your work overlooked. But now? Well, you know what I think. You have the ideal opportunity to promote your abilities as *yourself*. A young girl with a brilliant future . . . Consider it some more, I beg you.'

As the door closed quietly behind her friend, Georgiana did think about it. Deep down, she knew that everything Lucinda said was true. The irrational fear she felt was more to do with the humiliation she'd suffered since that dreadful day when she'd been found out. The reliving over and over again of the utter disbelief and despise in Christopher Merryfield's eyes was far more disturbing than the thought of the tedious journey to Yorkshire.

Her long, slim fingers smoothed the expensive paper that lay limply in her grasp. The request was reasonable. It was spelled out in black and white for her to see. Although he'd never before been aware that George Rankin even had a daughter, Joshua Merryfield was surprised and pleased to find that she had inherited his gift, which he'd thought considerable. He and Mrs Merryfield had been doubly amazed when they learned that Miss Rankin had taken a post teaching art and deportment at Lucinda Hargreaves' academy for young ladies. They were sorry to hear of the accidental death of George Rankin, and indeed the untimely demise of his young son who'd been his apprentice. Here, Georgiana paused for thought, wondering what they remembered about the 'young son'. She scoured the pages of the letter. No, there was no further reference to his name, no reference to 'Georgie'.

The only Merryfield who would possibly remember was Christopher — who, Georgiana had now learned from Jane, was known to family members, as Kit. So Kit might remember. But Kit wasn't going to be there.

If Kit was going to be there, she couldn't possibly consider it. Not even for an instant. But he wasn't. Jane had told her how disappointed they all were that he couldn't be home for Christmas, particularly his father who was in such poor health.

So? Should she go? Could she go? Dare she go?

★　★　★

Kit cursed the damp weather. Damp London weather in particular. Somehow rain in London was so much — well, *wetter*, and more penetrating than it was in Spain.

Spanish nights were damnably cold, of course, or could be. Nights spent camped on inhospitable soil, in a tent that was frayed and grey, on a lonely, narrow bed only inches from the ground; the familiar sounds of many men huddled together; the occasional spitting of a fire or fragments of a bawdy song drifting like smoke across the encampment . . . Spanish nights, bitterly cold, with only the camaraderie of the men for warmth.

Kit shifted in his seat and unconsciously put a hand to his left shoulder, which hurt like the devil in damp weather. The surgeon had done a good job of removing the ball he'd taken there, but the pain — usually dulled by brandy and warmth — which had come back to haunt him on his slow and ill-advised journey home tonight in London's damp was proving hard to extinguish.

He was spending the evening at his club, seated in a comfy leather chair before a roaring fire. It was the club that his fellow officers frequented when they were in town, but now that the war had ended — for good, this time — there were fewer officers around. At his elbow was a glass containing three fingers of brandy. He gave a taut smile and took a sip. On the whole, that was a good thing, wasn't it? If he were to sell his commission and go back to Yorkshire as his father so desired, then he'd have to get used to functioning alone.

He frowned, because that wasn't quite right, was it? His father was ill, by all accounts becoming frailer by the day. It was clearly his duty to go home to take up the reins of running the estate, interest himself in the farming and the Yorkshire way of life as once he had as a boy. His eyes clouded. But that was before. Before Arabella came along. Arabella, with her long lashes, lingering glances, low necklines and provocative manners. Arabella, who had twisted his widowed father round her little finger, along with every other member of the male sex with whom she came in contact.

The smile which crossed his features became momentarily bleak. Then he straightened his shoulders, grimacing as the left one gave another twinge. That was all four long years ago. He had changed in that time. Hopefully Arabella had too. Maybe she had settled down to domestic life now that her family were growing up. After all, Jane, his eldest half-sister, was sixteen now, and attending an academy in London; Elizabeth must be around thirteen, and little Josh nine.

Oh, to be nine again! Or, better still,

five! To be striding on the moors, alongside his father: his strong, tall, handsome father, who since his wife's death seemed to like nothing better than to devote his time and energy to his young son Kit.

But that was before Arabella.

When Kit was six, Arabella came into their lives, and once that happened Kit's father's priorities changed. For, as well as being beautiful, Kit found Arabella to be spoilt and wilful; cloyingly sweet to him when his father was in the vicinity, totally oblivious to him when he was not. He'd been confused and resentful in turn, Kit recognised this now. For the first time unsure of his place in life as well as in his father's affections, he did not take well to having a stepmother. No, he could not have been an easy child.

When the time came for him to be sent to school, he was pleased to go, and when he'd come home for the holidays he kept out of Arabella's way as much as possible, wandering over the estate, palling up again with the village lads he'd played with as a child. Life went on: never to be the same as when his mother was alive or before Arabella had become his father's second wife, but Kit knew himself to be privileged in many ways and was grateful for the fact. His little half-sisters were quite sweet, he supposed, but because of the age difference he didn't have much to do with them. And when baby Josh arrived — well, by that point, Kit considered himself to be a young man, and much too grown up to take an interest in babies!

And then had come the accident, the one that put his seemingly invincible father in a chair with wheels attached, and made of him a hopeless invalid, ever more to be dependent upon the strength of others.

To seventeen-year-old Kit, it felt like the end of the world. Although the countryside walks with his father had become increasingly rare, there would be no more of them. No more companionable rides over the mauve and brown shades of the moors, ever-changing in sequence with the scudding clouds overhead. No more fly-fishing, standing together, thigh-deep in brackish water, watching for the flash of a kingfisher. Kit had mourned for the loss of the father he knew best. For Joshua Merryfield had been an outdoors man, and had brought his son up to be the same. The fall from his horse had made of his once all-powerful, country-loving father, an indoor man. And the indoor territory of his home, to Kit, was now Arabella's province.

At first, he had borne it with as good a grace as he could muster. In the face of Joshua's sudden incapacity, Arabella and Kit had seemed to form some kind of truce; out of deference to his father, Kit was unfailingly polite and Arabella smilingly civil. But then, three months on, after the first shock had worn off, it became apparent that Joshua Merry-field was never going to walk again, and that his breathing would always be laboured. Arabella became bored.

Mutely, Kit had watched as Arabella gave parties and openly flirted with every man of her station that crossed her path. He watched as she arranged trips to the London house so she should be able to enjoy all that the metropolis had to offer. Initially, uncomplainingly, Joshua undertook these journeys — arduous as they must have been — saying that he refused to give in to the life of a recluse. But, quite soon, the sojourns to London became fewer, eventually reduced to perhaps the couple of months leading up to Christmas, and possibly taking in the spring season.

Then had come the day when Kit returned from school to find Arabella regarding him with a different look in her eye. It was a look which made Kit blush and stammer, a look he didn't care for, but which made him wonder about all kinds of possibilities that had never before crossed his mind. At least, not in connection with his stepmother.

The village girls, perhaps, or some of the above-stairs maids; but never in his wildest dreams his stepmother.

Arabella was bored beyond bearing. Kit knew that. She made no secret of it. Her temper frayed easily, she snapped at the servants, found fault with the children, and seemed to derive great amusement from making Kit feel uncomfortable.

She looked too beautiful; smelled too sweet; stood far, far, too close.

Every day became a contest for Kit, a fight between hate and desire. Shame, and a wanting that made him fling himself out of the house in the middle of the night; pick fights among the village lads with whom, it seemed only yesterday, he'd had so much in common. And it was all Arabella's fault: her fault for looking at him that way.

Oh, he hated Arabella all right; but he hated himself more.

The army seemed the only answer.

It had taken a lot of persuasion to

induce his father to agree; and had it not been for little Josh, who in recent months had earned a huge portion of his father's affection, Kit knew he would never have prevailed upon him to let him go. As it was, a commission was purchased and Kit set out for Spain.

He'd served well. Taken to the life, had all kinds of adventures and made some strong friendships. He'd taken part in more bloody skirmishes and battles than he would have liked, and had attended fewer balls and picnics and other entertainments than he'd hoped . . . but he'd learned a lot, always played fair, and behaved in a way which was expected of a gentleman. For four years he'd served, and now the war was over; he had taken a bullet, and perhaps it was time to go home to stay. But it was a huge decision. Could he settle again to the life of running the estate? Did he need to? For his father had often informed him that Arabella's cousin Hugo Ferdinand was doing a splendid job. He sighed; the choice between selling his commission or re-joining his regiment seeming impossible to make.

A log rolled from the fireplace. Kit contemplated kicking it back with his boot, but an attendant stepped forward and tonged it back into place in the large hearth.

Home! The very thought of it . . . Kit took another sip of brandy. He thought about Arabella, this time without the hot-headedness of youth. Surprisingly — at least, at the time it had been surprising — she'd been in favour of the enterprise. Perhaps even she had realised that to encourage any sort of relationship between herself and her stepson could be nothing but wrong. *Or perhaps*, thought the more mature and cynical Kit, *perhaps she thought that the chances of me being killed were high*. For if that had happened, then little Josh — who was, after all, of her own flesh and blood — would inherit his father's estate.

But he hadn't been killed. Despite his shoulder wound, he was very much alive; and suddenly the wildness of the moors, the thought of seeing his home and his father — and, yes, his half-brother and -sisters too — held an appeal that had started out as a whimsical notion only, but was fast turning into an impatient yearning.

Of course, he'd kept in contact with his father and sisters by letter, but had to admit to himself that the missives were more intermittent and brief than they should have been. It seemed the more time went on, the less he had to write about.

Thinking it might be possible to pay a brief surprise visit to them before possibly rejoining his regiment, he had not told them he would be in London at a time coinciding with their own planned Christmas visit to the town house, writing instead that the surgeon had advised against travel for the time being. Then had come the letter from Jane telling him that Papa's strength was failing, and although his dearest hope was to see Kit again soon, Joshua was unable to make the trip to London. *I have told him, as have you I am sure, it seems unmanageable for the time being,* she wrote. *For you are still in Spain nursing a wound which makes it impossible for you to travel, and there is much going on there even though the war is won. I shall however be travelling to Yorkshire myself, together with my teacher. Is not that the very best of things? For I quite thought I should have to go to Mama's relatives in London — which, although most agreeable, is not the same as being with one's family.*

So it seemed the so-difficult decision was already made. Instead of a surprise visit to the London house, he would travel instead to Yorkshire. But first he would arrange to sell his commission. Then he would hope for at least dry weather, and plan his journey.

He quaffed back his brandy and, as the heat from the fiery liquid spread through his body, relaxed a little into his chair and thought of the soft green valleys and purple-brown moors of Yorkshire.

3

The Yorkshire house was more of a mansion than anything Georgiana had ever considered could be described as a 'house'. In the main, she was used to the London town houses of the rich, although she had seen little further than the back stairs and the way through to the schoolroom, or somewhere else thought appropriate for an artist to work. The London houses were usually tall and many-roomed: there had been glimpses of elegance and extravagance — and, occasionally, examples of what her father called appallingly bad taste — but nothing that had prepared her for the scale of Markington Hall

After stopping overnight in a coaching inn on the outskirts of Leeds, they'd managed to arrive at the Hall before nightfall. En route, Georgiana had found herself recognising some of the scenery in the region of Harewood from the long-ago visit to Aubrey House. Although she had known Aubrey House to be the consequence of 'new money', she had thought it to be impressive. 'I'm not proud. Any money suits me,' Pa had said with a grin. And she felt her face soften and relax as, nostalgically, she thought of Squire Ashton's commission. It had been in summer, and the weather had been considered mighty warm by the locals; but to Georgiana, born and bred in London, even the summer air had felt fresh and distinctly chilly.

Her smile faded because in the present it was midwinter and bleak. She pulled the travel rug closer.

It seemed an everlasting journey, involving often uncomfortable overnight stays in unfamiliar coaching inns, but at last their carriage was turning in through ornate gates set in the York-stone wall which had marked their route on a rough, narrow roadway for the last couple of miles. At first,

Georgiana thought the large, solid-looking building that appeared about seventy yards to the right of the gates was their destination, and began to collect her muff and leather satchel together.

'Oh no, we're not here yet,' said Jane. 'That's the dower house, where Granny used to live.'

'Oh,' said Georgiana, eyeing the many windows of the substantial structure and thinking that Granny must have had a great many guests and servants to fill the rooms.

Climbing steadily upwards, the drive wound on. From time to time the trees planted either side allowed tantalising glimpses of old stone work, or the occasional turret, through their blackened winter branches. Then suddenly the trees stopped and Markington Hall was spread before them in full splendour.

Even on a December day it couldn't fail to impress.

Georgie held her breath in awe. *My,*

oh my, what would Pa have said to this?

It was grand. Although not huge on the scale of the Blenheim or Castle Howard palaces, it was grander than anything Georgiana had ever laid eyes on. Grander than any pictures she'd seen in books. Grander by far than Squire Ashton's Aubrey House, the only other northern building she'd been to.

The magnificent dwelling place was placed high on a mound, which Jane had told her was situated somewhere between Ripon and Harrogate. She was sure that on a clear day in the summer the house would be provided with stupendous views of the beautiful vale of York, the north Yorkshire moors a majestic backdrop in the distance. As it was, it stood proudly, its solid stone strong against the murky winter weather. There were lights in the windows: soft, welcoming candlelight. For the first time since embarking on this enterprise, Georgiana felt a glow of optimism and, as the initial shock of her first sight of Markington Hall wore off, she realised that Lucinda had been right in saying she would have been a fool to turn this opportunity down. She imagined Pa's expression if he could see her now. His eyes would be twinkling with glee; he would wink at her and tell her that this was a chance too good to miss. *Relish it, my love*, he would have said.

Her heart beat a little faster. If she made a good job of the painting her fortunes could change direction.

Georgiana's impression was that the building had first been designed and constructed in the late sixteen-hundreds, with extra wings and what was surely a quite recent addition of a large Georgian-type portico. Almost before the coach clattered to a halt, the high wooden doors at the top of the steps were flung open and, in a moment, the excited Jane had thrown herself out of the vehicle and was running up the stone steps and into the imposing hall. Georgiana followed at a more sedate pace, and arrived just in time to witness Jane being enfolded into the embrace of the most beautiful woman she had ever seen in her life.

Standing a little to one side of her Mama was a young girl of about thirteen years, who looked to have inherited her mother's beauty, and was taking her turn now to wrap her arms round her sister. On the other side, a boy of a few years younger was hopping up and down, trying to tell Jane about his newest puppy and that he might soon be allowed a new pony. It was a heartwarming scene, and one that did much to reassure Georgiana — who, after heaving a sigh of relief that to make the portrait acceptable she would not have to subtly flatter her subjects, smilingly stood in the shadows, waiting until the reunion should be over.

Eventually Arabella Merryfield turned towards her and held out her hands. 'And you must be Miss Rankin,' she said with a smile and a warm handclasp.

'I can't tell you how grateful we are that you escorted Jane home, and have accepted the challenge of painting us all . . . But for now, you must be exhausted, you poor thing. We'll have you shown to your room and your bags brought up. We dine at six. My husband likes to keep country hours, and you will meet him then.' After bestowing a charming smile in Georgiana's direction, she turned back to her eldest daughter. 'Now Jane, I know you can't wait to see dearest Papa. He is in the library, but I warn you he tires easily, so you are not to trouble him with too much of your chatter . . . Children, come with me!'

Georgiana returned the handclasp and nodded her head, wondering why she had ever questioned that she might like Arabella Merryfield; because, although being referred to as a 'poor thing' was something she wasn't quite sure she appreciated, her welcome far exceeded her expectations. Curiously, she examined her surroundings as she followed a stiff-backed maid up the sweeping staircase. Perhaps her sojourn in this amazingly grand house would be more enjoyable than she'd anticipated.

Her room, although situated on the north side of the building, was warm, due to the roaring fire laid in the grate and thick brocade curtains drawn against the cold. The furniture was old, but solid and well-cared-for, and her four-poster bed was soft and smelled of lavender. Georgie practically purred with satisfaction.

The maid, a country girl with a broad accent and a ready smile, pointed out the location of the new 'modern' water closet down the corridor, and told her that her bags and a jug of hot water for her use would be arriving shortly.

'I'll be back at five to help you dress, miss,' she said before backing deferentially out of the door.

Left to her own devices, Georgiana gave a wide grin, stretched her arms above her head and danced towards the bed. It was all she could do to stop herself jumping on it and laughing out loud. How fantastic! Her very own well-aired, luxurious, four-poster bed! It was soft and inviting, too. In fact, if she hadn't been so excited, she might have crept under the covers and fallen asleep straight away.

It was just as well she didn't, because there was a tap on the door and a footman arrived with her bags.

Oh Lord, she was expected to dress for dinner!

It was with some trepidation that she unpacked her bags. Along with change-able underclothes and chemises, she had brought her three best dresses and an old working dress of an indiscrimi-nate grey, over which she would wear her newest artist's smock. Examined now in her new environment, these hardly seemed good enough to make an appearance at her first dinner at Markington Hall.

Impatiently, she gave a shake of her shoulders. They wouldn't expect her to dress in the height of fashion. Surely they must guess that her clothes would be modest and — well, frankly, a little on the dull side. Her black gown of thick slub-silk, with satin ribbon binding at the neck and under the bust, was quite acceptable, she supposed. With a lace fichu in the daytime, or her mother's pearls in the evening — yes, it would pass muster in a paid-companion fashion, she thought. But maybe black for a first evening would be considered too formal, or too presumptuous — or just too black?

Perhaps the chestnut-brown merino wool would be better, with its discreet touch of braid under the bust, its high neck with interchangeable collars, and long, tight sleeves. Yes, she could wear her pearls, the only jewellery she possessed, or better still the seed pearl collar — pretty but unpretentious. She would dress her hair severely, so that only a few soft curls escaped on her neck, and she would appear the perfect teacher: a person of humble origin and modest tastes. Boring, but trustworthy; she was sure that would suit the

Merryfields perfectly.

On their journey from the south, Georgiana had learned quite a lot about the Merryfields. About Arabella who had been a well-known society beauty and had been swept off her feet seventeen years ago by Papa, a widower who had come to London in search of a new wife for himself and a stepmother for his son Kit.

It sounded to Georgiana, who had never really known her own mother, as though Arabella was a warm — if not very consistent — parent. Arabella loved to socialise; loved to dance and sing, attend picnics and balls, ride in the park, meet with her friends at the newest attractions, sport the most fashionable clothes, and indeed set a new fashion, maybe in the tilt of her hat or in dictating the exact shade of blue to be all the rage this season. She sounded passionate yet fickle, warm and loving . . . but with perhaps a streak of selfishness that kept her sweet when things went her way, but not so sweet when they didn't. On the whole, Georgiana thought she would be able to handle her.

'Of course,' said Jane against the swaying of the coach, 'it was devastating for poor Mama when Papa fell from his horse. It meant he could no longer escort her, you see. They could no longer live the life to which she'd become so accustomed. Papa used to say it was unjust to expect a rare exotic flower like Mama to live her life buried in the country forever.'

'Indeed.'

'At first, even after the accident, Papa used to accompany her to London or Brighton or wherever she was wont to visit, but sadly it became too much for him and he would stay in the country with us. He liked to be with his children, you see, and didn't mind that we were sometimes fractious or tediously boring . . . ' Jane paused and smiled. 'Mama's sensibilities were such that she couldn't abide it if one of us cried or was ill. It upset her so much she could hardly bear it . . . In some ways, we were very lucky — because, you see, it meant that we saw more of our Papa than most children do.'

Georgiana gave a cough. 'What about your brother?'

'You mean Josh? Oh, Papa dotes on Josh. He's nine now. Just at the age where Papa would love to go fishing and riding with him as he did with Kit, but of course he's unable to. But Josh understands, and is learning cribbage with him and all sorts of card games . . . And then there's Lizzie. She is very fair, like Mama: her hair is quite golden and she's so pretty, nearly as pretty as Mama. Papa calls her his little minx because she can twist him round her little finger. But Papa doesn't really have favourites. He loves us all, you see, quite dearly.'

Thinking of her own very dear Papa, Georgiana swallowed. 'It sounds as though you have a very happy family.'

'Oh, I do.' Jane's eyes sparkled. 'That's why I'm so grateful to you that you are escorting me home. We were so hoping that we would all spend Christmas together, and when things didn't work out that way, well . . . It was very disappointing, it's really so kind of you to put off your own plans to do this for us.'

Thinking of her nonexistent plans for the spending of Christmas, Georgie gave a thin smile. 'Oh, I wasn't doing so very much,' she said. 'And your parents are paying me handsomely for painting your portraits.'

'Well,' said Jane in what Georgiana recognised as a rare moment of insightfulness, 'Mama has asked for a family group of her with her children, so really it is four portraits of full-length figures, isn't it? It's a lot to ask.'

'I'm sure I shall enjoy doing it,' answered Georgie diplomatically.

'I did explain to Papa in a letter how very talented you are, and how you are particularly good at catching a likeness. I had no idea that your father painted the portrait of Kit that hangs in the town house! I think it's wonderful, but I never noticed the signature. I used to often stand and gaze at it, and I felt as though he was almost there with me.' She shivered theatrically. 'I sometimes think it was *meant* to be that you are here with me taking me home.'

'Oh, I think the coach driver has something to do with that too,' replied Georgie as they lurched over yet another rut in the road. 'But tell me, what of your stepbrother? I believe you call him Kit?'

'Well, he was away at school a lot and there are quite a few years between us, but he was always nice to me. He picked me up once after I had fallen out of a tree, and he carried me all the way home, singing to me to stop me crying. He had very bony shoulders, I recall. His eyes, too; I remember his dark eyes. Pa used to say he was like his mother, who was also beautiful, I believe, but not as beautiful as Mama.'

'Beauty comes in many different

guises, and one always thinks of one's mother as being beautiful.'

Jane sighed. 'We were all sorry when he went to war, but he was so determined that in the end Papa let him go. Then I suppose I just got used to it. So much else was happening, and he was so often absent anyway, that I didn't miss him as much as I should have. Papa always wrote, though; and so did I, because although his letters were short he always replied, and he did funny little drawings of stick men walking up hills and falling upside-down over the other side.'

Remembering the angry young man standing straight in his stiff new uniform, Georgie tried to imagine him drawing stick men in order to amuse his sisters. The scowling young man who had never really vanished from her mind somehow seemed more human, less intimidating. She wondered what he remembered of her.

A scrawny girl dressed as a boy, she thought. *A scrawny girl with nothing to recommend her at all.* 'Why should he remember me?'

She became conscious that Jane was looking at her with wondering eyes. 'Are you feeling quite the thing, Miss Rankin?'

Oh Lord, she'd spoken aloud.

'Yes, I'm quite well. I was just thinking of someone I used to know,' she lied hurriedly.

Jane's eyes shone. 'Was it a beau of yours when you were young?' she whispered.

Georgiana laughed. 'How old do you think I am, for heaven's sake?'

A fiery blush spread up to Jane's hairline. 'I'm sorry, Miss Rankin, only you seem too attractive to be a schoolteacher, so the girls . . . well, we all thought you might have had a sweetheart . . . '

'Ah, a grand romance? A grand passion? Sorry to disappoint you, but no; unfortunately, there are no secrets like that in my past. But — ' She leaned towards Jane confidingly. ' — I feel I still have some little time.'

Jane looked disappointed yet relieved, and seemed quite content to change the subject to her own family. But after that, Georgiana was somehow unable to bring the conversation back to the brother she was really interested in, and heard instead all about Josh who was growing so tall, about Jane's particular friend Prudence who lived near Harewood and whom Mama had promised to invite to stay for a few days at least. And about Uncle Hugo, who wasn't really an uncle but Mama's second cousin, who lived in the main house with them and acted as an estate manager in assistance to Papa.

'It is very lovely,' confided Jane. 'I never thought I would miss it as much. If the weather is good I will take you on my favourite walks, although there isn't so much to see in winter.'

Georgie's smile hid a shiver. The delights of the countryside were all very well, but in December?

Thinking of this now, Georgie examined her two pairs of boots and one pair of house shoes. The house shoes were exactly that — shoes that could be warn in the house but under no stretch of the imagination outside, where the walkways would undoubtedly be damp and slippery. She had a pair of walking boots with soles that were a little on the worn side, and a pair of newer boots which were much sturdier. But in typical generous style Jane had informed her she had a spare pair of pattens, the wooden soles on iron rings, which would keep her feet out of the mud ... at the thought of which, Georgiana shuddered, vowing to stay inside working as much as was possible.

Her attention went back to the clothes lying on the bed. Tonight, then, the chestnut-brown dress with the seed pearl collar and soft wool wrap that Lucinda had pressed upon her just before her journey, her house shoes and a discreet, but not too humble, smile.

By the time she had washed and half-dressed herself in front of the warm fire, Betsy the maid reappeared, and helped her to finish dressing and pin her hair into a softer style than her normal severe knot on the back of her head.

'Lovely hair, miss. So much of it, and a natural wave, and the colour . . . '

'Yes,' sighed Georgie. 'Carrots, I know.'

'It's beautiful, miss. They call it Titian!'

Gracious! Georgiana swallowed. Pa had always referred to her hair as *Titian*; fancy Betsy knowing such a term.

'Thank you, Betsy,' she said a moment later as the last hairpin went in. 'You have made a lady of me and I'm very grateful.'

Smiling, Betsy tidied the dressing table. 'No trouble, miss. The lady was already there, she was just hiding.'

'Thank you.' Betsy was very approachable, but somehow Georgiana resisted the urge to ask about the rest of the household. She would find out all in good time.

Dinner that evening, although not elaborate, was well-prepared and of richer fare than she was used to. First, she was introduced to Joshua Merryfield, who was already seated in his wheelchair at the head of the long dining table. There were four candelabras placed equidistantly along its length, but the family sat all together at one end. Of the children, only Jane joined them tonight, but a fair gentleman in his early thirties with even features and a ready smile was introduced as Hugo Ferdinand, Arabella's cousin twice removed and also acting estate manager at Markington Hall. He had a pleasing, open countenance, and Georgie gave him an answering friendly smile. Seated next to him was a tall lady with dark hair whose plain wool dress was as inoffensively forgettable as Georgie's. Her name was Miss Garvie. She gave a nod of the head and a brief twitch to the lips in Georgie's direction, and thereafter kept her eyes downcast.

Once they were all seated, Georgie

surveyed her fellow diners. The likeness between Christopher Merryfield and his father was only just detectable. There were lines of pain in Joshua's face, and his hair was greying at the temples, but the resemblance was there in the bone structure of the high-bridged nose and in the thin upper lip resting on the fuller, sensitive lower one. Joshua Merryfield had once been a very handsome man.

Just as she was thinking this, her eyes travelled upwards and met his piercing gaze, and she realised that she, in her turn, was under scrutiny.

'Hmm. You have a look of your father,' he barked suddenly. 'More serious, mind. George Rankin was always ready for a tall tale and a crack.'

'Yes, he was, sir,' said Georgiana, determined not to be nervous. 'He took life as it came and loved the challenges it threw at him. He enjoyed his life.'

'Hmm, had his share of misfortune too, I dare say. Wife's family disowned her for marrying beneath herself. Son

— pasty-faced boy as I remember — died young . . . that's a lot for a father to get over.'

'Indeed,' murmured Georgie, hoping he wouldn't dwell on details of the nonexistent son.

The scrutiny went on for longer than Georgie was prepared for, but she met his eyes steadily. She knew she'd never met him before, either as herself or as young Master Rankin. He couldn't know, he couldn't possibly know.

'Hmm,' he said eventually. 'You have a look of him. Let's hope you're as talented.'

'She is, Papa,' said Jane from beside him. 'You wait and see.'

Mr Merryfield picked up his spoon. 'What's this soup?' he enquired of no-one in particular. 'Not chicken broth, I hope!'

A mischievous glance passed between Jane and her mother. 'No, my love, it's Cook's best leek and potato, made with a sherry and chicken stock'

'Hmm' said Mr Merryfield, lifting his

spoon. Then, after a few mouthfuls: 'I could have gone to London, y'know, met up with Kit. I'm better now. Never been in better health! Would have liked to have seen him. Would've been worth the effort.'

'Joshua, you know Kit's still in Spain, he wasn't well enough to get to London anyway. And you know what Doctor Bainbridge said.'

'Doctor Bainbridge is an old woman,' said Joshua. 'He put me on chicken broth for a week ... Hmm! Lungs perfectly all right now. Perfectly.' He glared round, daring anyone to contradict him.

There was a long silence.

'The drainage pipes we put in the north field seem to be working,' said Hugo Ferdinand after a desperate glance at Arabella.

'Hmm!'

'It was on your advice, sir. And very good advice it's turned out to be, too.'

'Well, I've lived here all my life. Ought to know what I'm talking about.'

Dinner continued in this vein, with cover after cover being presented and removed, all conversation inclined for Joshua's edification and approval. But, casually glancing in his direction now and then, Georgiana was able to discern the very real affection for him emanating from around the table. She wondered how it must be for a strong and able man, in the space of a heartbeat, to be so cruelly confined to a wheeled chair for the remainder of his life. Once again, she felt grateful that at least Pa had been spared that.

After dinner, the ladies repaired to the withdrawing room, where Miss Garvie took out some embroidery and Jane and Arabella continued a conversation regarding the latest London fashions, to which sadly Georgie felt able to contribute little. After half an hour or so, Hugo arrived pushing Joshua's chair, which he directed to a place beside Arabella at the fireside. Having done this; he looked round and, bestowing a warm glance at Georgie, sat down beside her and endeavoured to engage her in small talk concerning the weather, how much she enjoyed her teaching job, and the extent of her artistic abilities.

'I always fancied myself to have a good eye,' he remarked. 'And I'm good at carrying a colour in my head. I learned a bit about it as a lad. The grinding of pigments, the colour-mixing — all that.'

'Really?' said Georgie politely. 'I tend to buy my pigments ready-ground these days, but . . . ' Her voice tailed off as there were sounds of a commotion from somewhere outside the drawing room doors. There was a slamming of wood on wood; the sound of boots on tiles. Then there were muffled but excited exclamations and noises of a swift passage upstairs.

'My God,' said a voice. 'What weather! I truly know I'm in Yorkshire now!'

Joshua Merryfield's face turned pale and his hand tightened on the arm of his chair. 'I'll be damned!' he said.

All eyes turned towards the door which was pushed open with a flourish.

'Papa!' In a trice the weather-worn yet undisputedly commanding figure that had appeared in the doorway had crossed the room to kneel at the side of the wheelchair. Joshua Merryfield's face had frozen halfway between shock and joy. 'Kit,' he said in a shaky voice. 'But let me look at you . . . Where are you hurt?'

'It's nothing. Took a ball in the shoulder. Damn nuisance, that's all.'

'They told me you couldn't get to London.'

'Well, I made them change their minds.'

'Kit, you're bleeding,' said Jane in a horrified voice.

Kit got to his feet. 'I apologise, Arabella.' His dispassionate gaze swept over her. 'Wasn't sure when, or if, I'd get here. Didn't want Papa high-tailing it down to London unnecessarily. Didn't mean to put you out. Last thing

I wanted to do. Your obedient servant, of course.' His eyes travelled to Jane, who was staring at his shoulder as though mesmerised by the darkening patch othere. 'Well, can this be my little sister Janey? Such a young lady, I hardly recognised you. Don't worry about the shoulder. Dressing's come adrift. My man'll fix it. Nothing to it, promise you. I'm right as a trivet.' In two strides he was at her side and lifting her with his good arm. 'I enjoyed your letters, every one of them. Thank you for writing. And — ' He took a step back his, eyes alighting on Georgiana. ' — who's this?'

Georgie wasn't a person who prayed regularly — only in church, and then only for form's sake — but now she sent a silent petition to anyone or anything that might have power enough to stop the next five minutes, when she would surely be exposed, from happening.

'I must apologise. Where are my manners?' said Arabella, who looked as stunned by the new arrival as everyone else. 'This is Miss Georgiana Rankin. She is Jane's teacher and she has come to paint our portraits.'

For the second time that evening, Georgiana found herself to be under intense scrutiny. Kit's astounded eyes looked into hers; at first searchingly, then with some vague recognition.

Georgiana lifted her head up and waited for the axe to fall.

4

'Well, I'll be damned,' said Kit.

He stared down into the cool grey eyes that were bravely, but fearfully, returning his gaze. It was the girl, the scrawny boy-girl, who had had the temerity to sketch him — and in a state of undress, too!

My God, that took him back. Back to that morning when he'd stood straight and proud in his new, slightly too big, uniform with its itchy collar. Back to the self-consciousness of being stared at by two pairs of searching eyes. Back to the excitement of knowing he was off to war, the youthful impatience to be on his way, and the fearful boredom of having to stand still for more than five minutes at a time.

More than four years had passed. But yes, it was her all right. Although how had she got here? What was she doing here? Why on earth, when he'd never expected to see her again, was she here in the flesh, staring at him with a look of anguished entreaty in her eyes?

Vaguely, he heard Arabella's voice in the background. 'I dare say, Kit, you hardly remember Mr Rankin — the artist who executed your portrait before you went to war?' He registered that it was said in the arch tone he'd once hated so much, but which no longer had the power to upset him. He continued to gaze at the slight female form before him.

My, oh my, but the girl had grown up to be — nothing, at first glance. But look again and she was — *arresting*, that was the word. Her hair was thick and luxurious and, pinned up as it was, appeared too heavy to be supported by her delicate neck. His eyes travelled on down, taking in her figure which, although slight, had charms that a severely-cut dress enhanced rather than hid.

'This Kit, is his daughter. She

teaches at the school Jane attends in London, and she was good enough to agree to accompany her home, and also to paint a family portrait of me and the girls.'

'I see.' Now he did see. Coincidence or not, Georgie — because he could in no way think of her as being Georgiana — was, it seemed, fated to cross his path again. Suddenly the humour of the situation made him laugh out loud.

'Forgive me,' he said, belatedly realising that all the occupants in the room were staring at him as though he had suddenly run mad. 'I'm glad to make your acquaintance, Miss Rankin . . . I apologise for my rag manners. I can only say that I am tired, and in need of some sustenance. I shall be better when I've eaten and rested.'

Immediately, both Jane and Arabella fussed round him, urging him to sit here next to dear Papa who was so very pleased to see him. Yes, he must sit beside the fire to warm himself. A tot of the best brandy was sent for, and a cut of meat along with pickles and cheeses were to be put on a tray for him.

Well, he was only human. Agreeing that he was indeed fagged to death, he sat back and basked in the welcome of his family. But whilst listening to his father grumbling on about fusty Doctor Bainbridge disallowing him from travelling, and in the next breath talking of drainage in the north field, he was aware of Georgie sitting discreetly in the background, hardly moving, as though scared of breathing, and how he had never been so pleased to see anyone in his life.

How could that be? He hardly knew her. Actually, he didn't know her at all, and in the normal turn of events never would do so.

He'd hardly spared her a thought over the last four years, but every so often, almost against his will, the image of her soft, full bottom lip, her direct grey eyes, and the unexpected river of red-gold hair tumbling from the boy's cap had flashed into his mind . . . but, just as quickly, had been pushed aside as the reality of war and life abroad took over.

She hadn't haunted his dreams by night, by no means! A chit of a girl, with little to recommend her — of what interest could she be to him?

But, all the same, she was here. Now. Here at Markington Hall — his home. Here, on the day of his arrival, giving him no time to reflect, no time to gather his forces. Only to feel her presence like an all-invading body blow.

And what had he done? He'd laughed like a hyena. Without a doubt, along with everyone else in the room, Georgie must think the war had addled his brain.

His father was looking at him with anxious eyes. It pained Kit to realise just how frail he had become. Playing his part, he smiled reassuringly and finished the brandy and his swiftly-prepared refreshment, all the while listening to his father's reminiscences, answering Jane's excited questions, exclaiming that he couldn't wait to set eyes on Lizzie and Josh, asking whether Prince was still in his father's stable, and thanking cousin Hugo for exercising him in his absence.

He was slightly surprised to find that, as well as Georgie the portrait-painter-cum-escort, Miss Garvie the governess had apparently been included in the family dinner. Arabella did not usually encourage any of the servants to attend family gatherings.

Intending to include the neglected-looking Miss Garvie in the reunion with the comment that she must have her work cut out trying to educate his younger siblings, he eventually sneaked a glance in Georgie's direction.

'No, indeed,' a flustered Miss Garvie was saying. 'They are very apt pupils.' Then, out of the corner of his eye, he could see that Georgie had risen from her seat which was a little out of the family group; and, with a whispered goodnight, was about to absent herself from the room.

'A fire is being lit in your old room tonight, Kit,' Arabella was saying, 'and your man Jenkins can sleep in your dressing room, in case you should need him.'

'Thank you,' said Kit. 'I intend on an early night; but tomorrow, Papa, we will have a long reunification, and you may tell me all the happenings at Markington. In return, I will try to inform you of what goes on in Spain. Sometimes, in spite of the war being over, I think these skirmishes will never end.'

Taking Georgie's lead, Miss Garvie also made to leave the room. 'I hope I'm not chasing you away,' he went on, rising to his feet. 'It surely wasn't my intention.'

'Miss Rankin and Jane have a tiring journey to recover from,' said Arabella quickly, 'and Miss Garvie never keeps late hours. Time for you to go too, Jane, you will see plenty of Kit tomorrow.'

Kit smiled and murmured a good-night to include both ladies and his sister, but his eyes were on Georgie. The entreaty not to give her away had been clear, but now the danger was over, it seemed she was prepared to behave as though they had indeed never met before. Her lowered eyelids didn't flicker as she turned to open the door and disappeared into the corridor.

'Seems like a sweet girl,' said Arabella, who was watching him through narrowed eyes. 'Whether she will be worth her fee remains to be seen.'

Kit said nothing.

* * *

Once Georgie reached the safety of her room, she leaned against the door with a sigh of relief. The worst had happened. That Kit had recognised her, she didn't doubt. But he'd kept silent, that was the important thing.

Would he continue to keep silent? Why should he? What advantage would there be for him?

She needed to stay in the background.

95

Move quietly. Speak only when spoken to, and do her job painstakingly and well. Yes, she could stay in the schoolroom where her equipment had been taken, claim to be a slower worker than her father. She could invent headaches and the need to take the air in order to avoid awkward questioning; generally make herself disappear. After all, it wouldn't be for long. The Christmas festivities would soon be over, the visit would come to an end, and, portrait completed, she would return with Jane to London. Surely she could manage for two weeks or so to play the talented, humble schoolteacher. Yes, she would manage.

Only when she had convinced herself of this would she allow her thoughts to stray to the tall, commanding, but exhausted young man who'd stood before her with uncomprehending shock in his eyes. The hollows around them showed he had seen too much warfare, but in spite of that he'd made the fatiguing journey north to see his ailing father. Surreptitiously observing him from the edge of the family circle, Georgiana had seen that there were echoes there of the nineteen-year-old boy he had been. His expression was still haughty until he smiled, when lines occurred in his cheeks and lights appeared in the depths of his dark eyes; but his frame had filled out, his thighs and torso broadened. Where there had been a boy, there now stood a man.

Georgie sat down on the nearest chair and put a hand to her burning cheek. Had she known he would arrive at Markington Hall, she would never have come; but now that she was faced with the prospect of spending some time, be it only a small amount, with him, what she felt was excitement, not dread.

There was a crackle as the firewood burned through and shifted in the grate. Georgie placed the last log onto the dying flames and set about undressing ready for bed.

'Show me the sketches.' Arabella sounded amused rather than demanding, but even so, Georgiana's hand shook as she drew the sketches from her satchel.

They were seated in the morning room where the thin winter sun filtered through, giving the illusion of warmth.

'I've sketched out two ideas for your consideration.' Nervously, Georgiana passed the two sepia sketches across to Arabella, who was looking particularly lovely this morning in a modish blue velvet gown. In contrast, Georgiana was wearing her drab work dress and her hair was drawn into a simple chignon at the back of her head. 'Please don't judge my skill from these. Preliminary sketches are only to place the subjects on the final canvas — to work out proportions and dimensions.'

'Well, yes, let me see,' said Arabella, who was looking hard at Georgiana rather than at the sketches which she held in her lap. Suddenly she sighed. 'We were not expecting my stepson to arrive last evening. No doubt all the commotion seemed a little strange and unsettling?'

An answer was expected. Georgiana drew her shawl a little closer round her shoulders. 'Not at all ... I have no family, so to me it was wonderful to see you all reunited despite ill health and injury.'

'I would have expected that he would give us forewarning.'

Oh, dear. Had she said too much?

'We had only set eyes on Kit once in the last four years, and that was a hurried occasion in London two years ago ... I must say, it seemed hardly worth it ... ' She gave the sketches a passing glance then looked up again at Georgiana. 'Mr Merryfield misses him very much, although we are all, of course, proud of him — it goes without saying.'

Georgiana's expression was carefully blank. 'Indeed.'

There was a short silence while Arabella turned her attention to the sketches. Georgiana breathed more easily. She was on surer ground discussing her work than the family affairs of the Merryfields.

'The first sketch is the standard formal study with all four of you looking straight out of the canvas at the viewer.'

Arabella said nothing.

'It has, until quite recently, been the accepted traditional way of presenting a family portrait; but I've also sketched a more modern, intimate pose.'

Arabella's eyebrows arched as she turned her head to see the second sketch.

'Please don't look for likenesses at the moment. It's the composition that's important. I think it would be quite charming to seat you, Mrs Merryfield, at the centre of the group, with Jane as the eldest standing slightly behind your right shoulder; and, as she has a delightful profile, looking down to her left and across you to where Josh is seated at your feet, glancing up as though he has just spoken. Elizabeth stands to your left, also looking across the scene, but I will catch her at three-quarter view.'

'And how will I be depicted?' asked Arabella, obviously unused to having her children's postures and attributes discussed before her own.

'Well, I can leave it to you to decide,' said Georgie with a smile. 'You are so beautiful from any angle it hardly matters, but I would like to group you just as I saw you for the first time, with you as the nucleus of a warm and loving family . . . '

'I see,' Arabella seemed to be mulling over the suggestion for a moment as though she couldn't quite find the compliment she had been expecting to lurk in Georgie's comments. 'I'll be in the middle, you say? Yes, I think I'd like that; although perhaps, if that is the case, all my children should be looking at me.'

Georgie swallowed. 'Of course, if that is what you would like.'

Arabella gave her a sharp glance. 'You don't agree?'

'I think it may appear a little, well — forced. You see, Jane and Josh, both being darker, compliment the composition by balancing and enhancing the fairness of Elizabeth and yourself, who are situated more towards the middle. If they all look at you, then they will all be in profile, their faces in sharper relief. They will appear softer and more natural looking at one another ... I think I would prefer you to be looking straight out of the canvas — surrounded by the love of your family, yes, but also showing your pride in them and their attributes.'

Hoping that Arabella would see the sense of her arguments, Georgiana held her breath. The truth was, children looking adoringly at their mother did not always make a convincing portrait. Too posed, too contrived by far.

'Well, it seems you've given this a lot

of thought,' said Arabella at last. She gave a tinkling laugh. 'I had no idea . . . I think I shall leave you to decide. Your idea of a relaxed family group sounds attractive. I think Mr Merryfield would like it. And, after all, we already have formal likenesses of us both here and in the London house. The one you are embarking on now will remain here at Markington, so my husband may be reminded of us when we are absent.' Arabella cast her eyes once more over the proposed sketches, lingering longer on the less formal of the two. 'Yes, I think it will suit very well,' she said.

Georgie was disappointed So the portrait would not be hung in pride of place in the London house, giving the elite every opportunity of seeing it. Perhaps she should have stuck with the idea of a boring formal pose after all. Well, her only option was to make such a good study of the Merryfield group that Arabella might decide on another more formal portrait for London. That would be perfect indeed!

Arabella rose to her feet. 'Perhaps we could have the first sitting this afternoon. The children will be less excitable then, and I will also be available. I expect you have some preliminary work to do. I'll have your luncheon sent to the schoolroom. Although they have no lessons today, the children will eat there with their governess, and it would be fitting if you joined them.'

Almost faint with relief, Georgiana gathered her things together. 'Thank you, Mrs Merryfield, for making me so welcome.'

With a swish of her skirts and a slight inclination of her head, Mrs Merryfield left the room.

★ ★ ★

The wind was cold, but it was good Yorkshire air. Kit sniffed appreciatively.

'Need a leg up, coz?'

Apart from the fact that Hugo could only in loosest of terms be considered his cousin, the query was unnecessary, thought Kit. A group of admiring stable lads had already collected in order to assist the returned wounded hero in mounting. Nevertheless, he nodded to Hugo, who was already seated on a heavily-built chestnut hunter, ruffled the hair of the sturdiest stable boy within reach, and was very soon seated on Prince, the favourite and steadiest of his father's horses.

'Just a steady hack,' he said quietly. 'I shall be in trouble with Jenkins if this wound opens again.'

Hugo leaned forward with friendly concern. 'You look far from robust. You're sure you want to do this?'

He was rewarded with a sharp glance. 'I shouldn't have suggested it unless I were sure. The weather is set to change, I believe, either tomorrow or the next day, and then I would be sorry to have missed this opportunity.'

Maybe in a few weeks he would risk tackling the open ground, which was badly rutted where the soil had been waterlogged then frozen in turn; but for now that was not to be, and he'd have to stick to firmer terrain. Slowly, Kit walked Prince, who he had been gratified to find remembered his old master perfectly, out of the stables and onto the well-remembered bridle path. The track bypassed the formal gardens, wound its way through the parklands, and was the best way to view the immediate surrounding estate.

'It seems Papa rarely appears before noon,' he observed to Hugo when they had skirted the meadow.

'You have the right of it,' answered Hugo shortly. 'You cannot fail to have noticed a change in him.'

Other than an involuntary frown, Kit saw no need to reply, and instead asked questions pertaining to the estate and the previous harvest; the number of head of cattle and sheep; the state of the farm workers' cottages; and even the method of new drainage installed in the north field.

The ride, which was only to take in a fraction of the estate, had been planned to last two hours at the most, but instead took three. Hugo was in favour only of nodding briefly when any casual estate worker was encountered along the way, but Kit — although excusing himself from dismounting, on account of Jenkins' wrath — exchanged pleasantries with them all, finding to his surprise that he was able to recall names with no prompting.

When eventually they turned towards home he found he was experiencing a pleasant sense of weariness; and, unexpectedly, an overriding feeling of belonging.

'Why are you smiling?' asked Hugo.

'Am I? Well, I suppose because I find the place so little changed and so well looked after,' replied Kit, his smile stretching further. 'And, my friend, I think that you are largely the one I have to thank for that.'

Hugo turned in his saddle and regarded his cousin through candid eyes. 'Your father pays me well. Besides, I love Markington . . . No thanks are required. I'm allowed to make decisions that in any other circumstances would be forbidden me. I'm well satisfied with my lot — I assure you.'

'Even so,' said Kit after a moment, 'I've been away a long time . . . ' He narrowed his eyes against a weak sunbeam that managed to slant its way through a dull cloud. 'Too long.'

Hugo gave him a sideways glance. 'How extended will your stay be? I imagine you will be rejoining your regiment before the spring?'

On the verge of telling him that, in that case, he imagined incorrectly, Kit checked himself. No, he should first discuss this with his father. Proceed slowly and carefully. Hugo had obviously become used to being the man in charge at Markington; it would be foolish to upset him.

'The family all seem well,' he said instead. 'I'm looking forward to being with them. Jane, I feel I know from before I went away, and from her letters. Lizzie, I know less of. The little

I've seen of her reminds me of her mother. Josh seems like a sparky little chap, enthusiastic about his animals if not his lessons. I must get to know them all again.' He paused. 'Arabella is in good looks, as ever. She hardly seems to have changed. Except perhaps she is more content now with country living?'

'Jane, when she's here, is good company for her now she's older,' answered Hugo blandly. 'And, speaking of good company, that little dab of a painting teacher she has brought with her . . . I expected her to be as plain as a pikestaff, but she's quite a taking little thing, wouldn't you say?'

Kit pretended to consider. 'In a quiet way,' he said eventually. 'Although with all that was going on and my shoulder throbbing to high heaven, I hardly noticed.'

'Oh? I thought from your reaction you might have met before.'

Kit treated him to a penetrating glance. 'Now, why on earth should you think that? I've been in Spain for most of the last four years.'

'Well, you did stare rather.' He shrugged. 'Just an impression I picked up.'

'Truth is,' Kit lied. 'I was so bamboozled, I thought for a moment she was someone I ought to know but didn't recognise. Maybe another distant cousin I knew of only vaguely.' He smiled disarmingly. 'After all, you are Arabella's second cousin, are you not? How do I know she doesn't have another?'

After looking at him oddly for a moment, Hugo said nothing, and they continued their way to the stables.

'Thank you for accompanying me. I should have managed alone, but it was good to have company.'

Immediately, Hugo was all affability. 'Nonsense, I enjoyed it, coz. I only hope your wound has endured the exercise.'

With help from Hugo, who held on to Prince's bridle, Kit gingerly dismounted then stood watching as Hugo rode on to the stables, leading Prince and shouting to the stable boys to look lively because here were two horses ready for a rub-down.

Yes, the sooner Kit made his plans known, the better it would be for all concerned.

★ ★ ★

Once the ice was broken, luncheon in the schoolroom was a comfortable affair. Miss Garvie although not easily given to voicing her own opinions, only those of her late dear mother or her employers, proved to be an undemanding companion, and Jane and Lizzie chatted effortlessly. Young Josh rolled his eyes a few times when talk turned to the Portuguese lace and hair combs that Kit had brought home, and he soon excused himself in order to visit the stables and check on the new young puppies.

'D'you think Kit might like to come with me?' he asked Jane. 'He likes dogs. Told me so this morning.'

'Kit is lunching with Papa at present, but perhaps another day. Or you could ask him later when the sitting's over.'

Miss Garvie looked alarmed. 'Take care not to get grubby,' she said, 'and you have only half an hour to see those puppies — don't forget your Mama will be here by then.'

'I can manage without him for a while,' said Georgie smiling. 'And at this stage, it really doesn't matter whether or not he's dirty ... ' She caught Miss Garvie's eye. 'On the whole, *not* dirty would be best, though. For the preliminaries, I'm only interested in shapes — children can't be expected to sit still for too long.'

The escaping Josh gave her a cheeky grin over his shoulder. 'Jane said you weren't the sort to prosy on.'

The remains of the meal were cleared away and Lizzie and Jane made a great business of tidying themselves. Miss Garvie chose this moment to withdraw in order to write letters.

The painting was to be of moderate

size, to fit in a particular alcove. Whether or not it would remain there would depend upon how much it pleased her patrons. With this in mind, Georgie set up her easel with some drawing paper clipped to a board.

'I thought it would be on canvas,' said Lizzie with a note of distain in her voice.

'It will be, but first I must plan my picture. I must see your shapes in relation to one another and place them within the square.'

'Oh,' said Lizzie looking bored. 'Will it take a long time?'

'I am normally held to be a speedy worker,' replied Georgie. 'But don't worry, if you are tired you have only to say. I have a rough idea already of how I would like you to pose.'

'Surely Mama will be the one to decide that.'

Georgie felt a flash of annoyance. 'Your mother and I have already discussed the pose, Lizzie.'

There was a rustle of skirts outside

the door and on a waft of perfume Arabella walked in.

She gave a charming smile. 'Oh good, you're ready, Miss Rankin. I've managed to come earlier than planned. I thought you might like to use the light while it lasts.'

'Thank you, that was most thoughtful.' Georgie continued to arrange her materials. 'I've had the couch placed opposite the window where my easel is standing, so that I can use the light on my work and also on the family group . . . That's perfect,' she went on as Arabella adeptly seated herself so as to be at the centre of the group.

Georgiana staged Jane and Lizzie in position, and explained where Josh would be seated on the floor.

'Yes, where is Josh?' asked Arabella with a frown.

'Miss Rankin said he could go to the stables and play with the puppies first,' said Lizzie with a smirk.

'No, *I* did,' Jane intervened quickly. 'He promised to be back soon.'

'Oh,' said Arabella, not looking best pleased. 'Well, I hope he's quick. I don't want to be here all day.'

'If I could ask you all to adopt a pose which feels comfortable and natural . . . ' said Georgiana. 'And Jane and Lizzie, if you could look towards where Josh will be sitting, so that I can gauge the rough position of the angles of the heads . . . Mrs Merryfield, you are just perfect as you are. Don't try to keep any particular expression on your face; that will all come much later. I'm just concentrating on lines at the moment.'

The sitting started. Eventually Josh burst in, pink in the face and slightly grubby round the edges, but he swiftly took up position, only asking once if Mama didn't think it a good idea to include the new puppy, who was very jolly, and he was sure would keep still for long enough.

'Dear heart,' said Arabella, her expression softening as it always did when she looked at one of her children. 'He's not house-trained yet.'

After adjusting the girls' arms and hands so that they appeared elegant, yet were relatively easy to draw — after all, why make life hard for herself? — Georgiana worked rapidly. She found that, compared with the first sketches she'd made from memory and imagination only, Jane was taller, and Lizzie slimmer. Josh managed to look totally adorable even with a scowl, which she couldn't help but see as a replica of his brother's when asked to keep still for a likeness to be taken, four years ago. Adjustments were made: Jane further forward, Lizzie more to the right, and Georgie gave Josh slightly more importance when it came to the light, hoping Arabella would accept the changes, small as they were.

She needn't have worried. When the sitting was over, the only one to show any interest was Jane. Intent upon their own business, the others went immediately. After some admiring comments Jane also left, leaving Georgie to pack up her equipment alone.

Crouching in order to mark the wooden floorboards with chalk where her easel stood, ready for the next sitting, she heard the door open behind her. Thinking it was probably Miss Garvie, she didn't straighten immediately. 'I won't be a moment,' she said. 'Then I'll be out of your way. Oh, and please could you leave the couch exactly as it is until the next . . . ' Her voice petered out as she straightened and turned. 'Oh!'

'Yes, *oh* indeed,' said Kit, looking her up and down as though pleased with what he saw.

Georgie felt her face flood with colour. He stood tall and straight and undeniably handsome. Despite their tiredness, his eyes held a warmth that crept through her guard and made her smile.

'Thank you,' she said softly.

He looked genuinely puzzled. 'What for?'

'Not giving me away.'

Now a grin appeared. 'Don't know

what you're talking about . . . Never set
eyes on you before in my life. Difficult,
though. What was your brother's name
again?'

'We could call him Tommy, if you
like.'

'Georgie — Tommy? Yes, that might
answer.' His eyes swept the room. 'I
came here expecting to share a
schoolroom tea and get to know my
siblings again.'

'In that case, you have a good forty
minutes to wait. We've just finished the
first sitting, and your sisters and
brother couldn't wait to get away.'

She was standing in front of the
easel. Kit crossed the room. 'Might I
look?' he asked, stooping slightly to
peer at her work.

Hastily, Georgie moved to one side,
and as she did so caught her foot on
one of the easel legs. The board tipped
drunkenly, wobbled a bit, then — disas-
ter — crashed against Kit's shoulder!

Wincing with pain, he doubled in
two.

'Oh no, your poor shoulder. I'm so sorry.'

Kit staggered to the couch and sat down, his face turning an interesting shade of pale. Without thinking, Georgie sat beside him and lightly stroked his good arm. 'Should I get you some water? You look a little faint.'

'My own clumsy fault . . . Don't look so scared. I'll be better directly. A stiff brandy wouldn't come amiss, though.'

Georgie looked wildly round the schoolroom.

'No, my sweet, you won't find any here. Good of you to look, though.'

Immediately, Georgie stiffened. He'd called her his *sweet*. How dared he? Eyes blazing, she looked towards him to find him regarding her through amused eyes.

'Still got your temper, I see. That's good. Don't become too buttoned-up, my little firecracker . . . Never fear, I won't call you 'my sweet' again — although I must confess I find the idea attractive.' He lifted his finger and slowly drew it from her eyebrow down the line of her cheek to her throat. 'Oh yes, I find the idea very attractive indeed.'

Somehow, Georgie managed to get to her feet. 'Sir, you mistake me,' she said. 'I am a schoolteacher and, when the opportunity arises, I paint portraits . . . I am not here to be made fun of — or, in fact, for anything else that might be in your mind.'

A trifle unsteadily, Kit attempted to rise to his feet, then sank back down again. 'I think I'll stay here until tea arrives,' he said. 'Brandy would be infinitely better, but tea would do.'

Georgie continued her contemplation of him, then she collected her pencils and sketchbook, draped a cloth over her unfinished work, and shifted the easel against the wall where it would be out of the way. 'I'll see if I can find someone to bring you some brandy,' she said.

Luckily enough, there was a footman at the end of the corridor. 'Mr Kit is in the schoolroom,' she said. 'As tea is not yet served, he expressed a desire for brandy.'

The footman looked at her blankly. She licked dry lips. 'I think his wound is troubling him, but he doesn't want a fuss,' she added.

The footman nodded and hurried away.

Georgie put a hand to her cheek, where the touch of Kit's finger still burned, and decided she would miss tea and retire to her room until dinner.

5

Dinner was another dilemma. Was she expected to attend with the family again, or to assume that last night was an exception and that tonight she was to dine with the rest of the above-stairs staff in the housekeeper's dining room? It was all a problem, together with what to wear — all over again!

When she'd agreed to come here, she'd never imagined it could possibly be so complicated. At other homes of the gentry she'd visited with Pa, the terms had been laid out clearly. The two of them were either included in the family gatherings — much as a lady companion or tutor might be — or not. Judging from her only other experience of the Merryfields — no unnecessary fraternising with the family, the meagre lunch tray — Georgie had assumed that 'not' would be the likely setup. Last night had been unfortunate, really, because taking her meals with the above-stairs staff would have suited her very well. How could she now sit at the family table and eat, all the time terrified Kit might say something to give her away?

With her head spinning, Georgie lay down on her bed, trying hard not to remember the touch of Kit's hand, the warmth in his expression. He was gentry, she was not. There was no point in her getting any romantic ideas about him.

In the end, she took out the chestnut dress again, but instead of the seed pearl collar this time she chose the lace. By the time a flustered Betsy arrived to help fasten her gown and fashion her hair, Georgie had herself under control enough to listen to the maid's natural chattiness, which required nothing more than a few nods or shakes of the head as an answer.

'Sorry I'm a bit late, miss, there's a sight more to do what with Mr Kit here, and him turning up out of the blue like that. He remembered me too, and I was only a housemaid then — before he went, I mean. He's a proper gentleman.' Her already pink face flushed a little more. 'Just like his father. Tomorrow, now, we're having guests for dinner. The master wanted to put them off, what with Kit coming home and all, and neither of them being robust, but no, Mrs Merryfield would have none of it; so we have four to stay over for three days, plus the vicar and the doctor and his wife for dinner — they're local, so at least no beds required. Oh yes, you're to be included too, together with Miss Garvie and, of course, Mr Hugo . . . Of course, in the country, Mr Merryfield has always kept a friendly house. No high-stickler ways about him, oh no! In town, though, it's a different story, Mrs Merryfield has her way there, and you and Miss Garvie would be kept very much below-stairs.' After a telling nod, Betsy pursed her lips as though she'd said too much.

'Do the visitors include a Miss Prudence?' asked Georgie, bending her neck so that Betsy could attend to a stray lock of hair. 'I believe she is a particular friend of Jane's — she was looking forward to seeing her.'

'That's right,' said the lady's maid. 'Miss Prudence, and her brother Charles.' She twisted Georgiana's hair into a knot and reached for extra pins. 'Miss Prudence has very thick hair too, but it's rather mousey. I don't know whether I'll be helping with her toilet or if her mother's maid will do both. We'll have to see ... I just hope all this excitement won't be too much for Mr Merryfield. He has his gruff ways, but I don't like to see him knocked up. He goes a dreadful colour and his breathing's something awful.'

'Betsy, with all these extra jobs ... although I love the way you do my hair, honestly, I've been attending to myself all these years. You don't have to attend to me when time is short.'

She was treated to a penetrating glance. 'You're alright, miss. I like doing your hair — everyone deserves a bit of pampering now and then. You bringing Miss Jane home was a nice thing, otherwise she'd have had to stay in London with Mrs Merryfield's family, and I doubt she'd have liked that!' She gave a final pat to Georgie's hair. 'Beautiful, really beautiful!'

Imagining her saying this at the finish of every lady's toilet, Georgie smiled her thanks.

'Now, give it a bit longer before you go down. Miss Jane is done, and Miss Garvie needs doing — but she's sensitive, and I don't like to upset her by her knowing I've done you first.'

'Of course,' said Georgie, feeling well and truly done, and barely able to keep the amusement out of her eyes.

Dinner that evening turned out to be a quiet affair. Most of Kit's attention was focused on his father, with only occasional teasing comments to Jane and questions concerning the estate to

Hugo, who answered placidly enough. Opposite her, Miss Garvie was, as ever, silent unless spoken to; even so, Georgie struggled valiantly to engage her in a conversation concerning embroidery, about which she knew little. Arabella was seated on her husband's left, and tonight her cousin was placed between her and Georgie. Most of Hugo's time was monopolised by Arabella, who was probably feeling a little put out by the obvious closeness between the reunited father and son. To Georgie, her laughter seemed just a little too forced, a little too bright.

Food came and went. More relaxed by this time, Georgie tucked in, and took several sips of the unfamiliar wine. She thought maybe it was a taste she could get used to, and was on the point of accepting a second glass when she looked up and met Kit's glint of amusement from the top of the table. Hurriedly, she put her hand over her glass in the way she had seen Miss Garvie demur. *Oh yes, Georgie,* she told herself, *you can act every inch the lady*.

'How are you progressing with the portrait, Miss Rankin?' asked Hugo as Arabella turned away from him in order to answer a comment from her husband.

'Well enough,' she replied. 'I've placed the figures today, and I have a fair notion of the way in which I want the study to be perceived.'

'And how is that?' He sounded genuinely interested.

'As a family group. But a relaxed family group. An informal study of a happy household.'

'You are fortunate in that the family share such good looks.'

'Indeed,' agreed Georgie. 'You can't imagine how my heart leapt when I first set eyes on them.' She became aware of Arabella's tinkling laugh, and realised that her attention had come back to Hugo and she'd been privy to her last remark. 'I have to hope I can do the Merryfields justice,' she added. 'I surely will try my best.'

There. If that didn't win Arabella over, nothing would.

From the other side of Hugo, Arabella smiled and tapped his arm in order to regain his sole attention. 'I look forward to seeing the painting when it's finished. At the moment, all one can make out is a series of lines and curves on cartridge paper. Hopefully, as time goes on, a canvas and paints will be produced and the portrait's progress will become more interesting.'

'My habit is to keep my pigments safely out of reach until I need to mix them,' said Georgiana, with a smile she hoped wasn't too saccharine. 'Some of them are quite toxic.'

'Heavens,' said Arabella. 'And I thought paint was made from earth and clay and vegetables.'

'It is — in a manner of speaking. Some pigments are from fairly harmless sources, some from minerals and other quite dangerous substances.'

Arabella gave a theatrical shiver.

'Well,' said Hugo diplomatically, 'I'm sure the portrait will be beautiful, whatever the materials used in its execution.'

At that moment Joshua, who was at the head of the table, sat back in his chair, looked around at the other diners, and tapped a fork against a glass.

'Hmm,' he began, scrutinising them all from beneath bushy eyebrows. 'I have an announcement to make . . . ' He paused for dramatic effect and his eyes travelled slowly from face to face.

Georgie held her breath. They'd found her out. That was what it was. Once she'd made it plain to Kit that she was not to be trifled with, despite his promise, he had told his father her secret, and now he was about to berate her in front of his family and dismiss her from his employ.

She knew she shouldn't have come! She should have listened to the innermost voice which had warned her that this whole enterprise could end in nothing but tears.

Trembling slightly, she fixed her eyes onto Miss Garvie's small silver cross, which just showed above the lace modesty panel in the V of her neckline.

'It gives me pleasure to announce . . .' said Joshua Merryfield, ' . . . no, great . . . no, *huge* pleasure, that my son — that is, Kit . . .'

Georgie lifted her eyes. Oh, so Kit was going to get married, that must be it. Her heart sank like a stone. Well, it was obviously not before time. It would be to some gentrified creature with the pedigree of a racehorse and a face to match. And, after all, an announcement of Kit's forthcoming marriage was surely better than the whole family knowing what a fraud she was.

Georgie breathed again. Good, this was good. She rescued her smile from cold storage ready for display.

An enormous grin split Mr Merryfield's face as he turned towards his son. 'Kit, my boy — is home for good! He's sold his commission, and he intends to spend time in getting to know the estate again. He is going to take over the reins of Markington Hall ... ' His eyes, which were suspiciously bright, swept the room once more. 'Wonderful news, hey?'

There was a small silence, only broken when Jane squealed with delight and, leaning sideways, flung her arms around her brother's neck. 'Oh, Kit, to think I won't have to worry about your getting killed ever again!'

'Steady on,' said Kit, looking pleased all the same.

Quite overcome at seeing the genuine affection radiating between brother and sister, Georgie's eyes filled with sudden tears at the renewed realisation of how totally alone she was. No parents, no siblings. She looked at the other faces around the table; without exception, all heads were turned towards Kit.

If Arabella was shocked and not best pleased at learning the news in this surprise fashion, she hid it well; she was smiling fondly at her husband, who was gripping her by the hand.

Even though no one was listening to her, Miss Garvie was twittering away in a congratulatory manner, and Hugo — Hugo was staring at Kit as though he could hardly believe what he had just heard. Covertly, Georgie watched as Hugo recovered himself, forced a smile, and rose from his feet in order to shake Kit's hand.

'Well done coz,' he said wringing Kit's hand up and down, up and down, in a manner that had Georgie worrying for Kit's sore shoulder. 'Hardly dared hope, old chap, but it will be grand to have you on board.'

Kit grinned back. 'On board? Not sailing anywhere, are we?' he joked. 'Won't want to tread on your toes, of course, Hugo; as I was saying to you earlier, you've been doing a marvellous job here, and I'm looking forward to helping you out, conferring with you . . . well, you know the sort of thing.'

'Hrmph!' Mr Merryfield cleared his throat. 'I'll take this opportunity to add,' he started, 'that Hugo has done splendidly here at Markington. In order to show my gratitude, I am giving him one of the properties on the estate where he can make his own home and continue, of course, in his role as estate manager.'

'Too kind, sir,' said Hugo, rather white-faced. 'But, I assure you, unnecessary. I am quite happy with my rooms in the west wing over the estate office.'

Mr Merryfield's rather fierce eyebrows drew together. 'I wasn't suggesting you move out tonight, Hugo, but Kit will be using the rooms over the estate office — in fact, the whole of the west wing — for himself. Only fitting, you know; my son and heir and all that. Besides, want him near me. And you, boy, you'll be wanting your own life. It's the cottage — five bedrooms, servants in the attic, own garden — down by the lake; a man can be private there. Hmm? Given you your own place, so you can set up house yourself. Look round for a wife. You know the sort of thing.'

Hugo smiled and stretched out his hand. 'Thank you, sir. You're most kind, but then you have always been generous to a fault.'

At a sign from Mr Merryfield, Brewer the butler, who'd been standing back pretending to be part of the furniture, moved forward carrying a silver bucket containing a bottle of champagne.

Amongst all the *oohs* and ahs as the champagne was opened and poured, Georgie thought that she was probably the only one who saw Hugo turn his eyes in Arabella's direction, or noticed the bleakness in their expression.

★ ★ ★

Kit was used to rising early and old habits die hard. So here he was on a cold, dreary December morning, wide awake, dressed and hungry, long before the other occupants of the place were stirring. Apart from the servants, of course. They'd been up since dawn.

Visitors were expected today, and Kit knew the drill. Avoid Arabella's contradictory instructions and the ensuing chaos at all costs. His best bet was to breakfast early and find his favourite wing-chair before a roaring fire in a comfortable corner of the library. Then later, if the mood took him, he'd drop in at the schoolroom and see what was going on there. Maybe there'd be lessons, or maybe Georgie would be there in her plain calico work dress — which, despite being nondescript, fitted her rather well, he'd noticed. If the others were there for a sitting he might observe her work for a bit, if she didn't object; or then again, he might still watch even if she did. He rather liked annoying her. Liked to watch the sudden fire come and go in her eyes. He remembered the stillness of her too, when she was working: the concentration that emanated from every pore. He liked that as well.

But first, he quietly let himself out of his room and walked soft-footed down the corridor, intending to use the back staircase down to the ground floor, where he'd find outdoor clothing in the boot room, whistle for any dog who cared to accompany him, and take a brief walk round the perimeter of the main house before his quest for breakfast.

In order to reach the nearest back stairs, he had to pass the west wing. Just before he reached the small landing, he heard the creak of the hinge to the door of Hugo's apartments. So Hugo was up too. He'd have to get that hinge oiled before he moved in.

Then he stopped mid-tread.

There was the unmistakable swish of skirts and a trace of perfume, something French and undoubtedly expensive, wafted to his nostrils. Cautiously, he peered round the corner.

Her back to him, Arabella was stealthily intent on closing the door with no further sound. Her hair was mussed, her face flushed, and she was wearing a peignoir fashioned in rustling silk — over little else, as far as Kit could tell.

He stepped back into the shadows. So, Arabella was still up to her little games, was she? Surreptitiously he watched as she quietly made her way to the back stairs and slipped down them. He imagined she'd make her way to her own apartment via the back passages and the children's quarters: she probably knew her way blindfolded by now.

No longer the inexperienced youth he used to be, although a part of him was furious on behalf of his father, another part of Kit held a certain sympathy for Arabella, who had hardly expected to find her married life so sorely interrupted by the tragedy that had left his father an invalid.

And what of Hugo? Kit allowed himself a smile at his own stupidity. Of course, he should have guessed at the outset how it would be. Although older than Kit, Hugo was still a young man; good-looking, healthy, and, above all, available. He probably never stood a chance.

So who was it hurting? As long as she was discreet ... probably no one. The servants, if they were aware, would never presume to comment. For a moment Kit felt sad, wondering whether Papa knew and was putting a brave face on it. Well, that was something he'd never know for sure, and he was glad that was the case. He certainly wouldn't be the person to inform him.

Whistling just loudly enough to make anyone else who was an early riser aware of his presence, Kit continued down to the boot room, managing in some mysterious way to alert two lurchers, a spaniel, and a labrador in the process. He shrugged his way into an old riding coat, which he dimly remembered as once belonging to his father, and his own well-worn boots. Then, after a more piercing, dog-calling whistle, in case there were any more around who were longing to go out and wanted company, he let himself out of the back of the Hall.

My, but it was cold today. He'd expected a damp cold, the sort that made his shoulder ache to high heaven, but it had altered overnight to a crisp chill, the dampness now a bitter bleak.

Sniffing at the change in the weather, the dogs ran ahead. Kit's boots scrunched on the gravel underfoot and his eyes narrowed against the cold as he thought again about cousin Hugo, who he'd barely heard about before he'd taken up residence as estate manager a few years ago. That he was indeed a distant cousin of Arabella's, he had no doubt. Everyone had distant cousins they didn't know much about. Possibly Arabella had come across him on one of her forays to town during the season. Maybe he'd been looking out for a rich wife — or an easy job. Kit's brow wrinkled — no, that was hardly fair: from all that he'd seen so far, Hugo had been worth his weight in gold. Papa's letters, arriving a little irregularly whilst

Kit was abroad, had always indicated that affairs at Markington were going well; and Papa, although an invalid, was no fool. He might not be able to tour the estate physically, as he'd have preferred, but Kit knew he kept a keen eye on the estate ledgers and spoke at length to his tenants when they visited the estate office.

It must have been a nasty surprise to Hugo when it was announced that Kit had sold his commission and was home for good. He'd disguised it well too, thought Kit. Especially the shock of finding he was to lose his rooms in the west wing, and be given a property three-quarters of a mile from his cousin Arabella.

Well, Kit could hardly help it if Papa expected him to move back to Markington. It was, after all, his home. Anyway, he wanted it too, and if he was to have the west wing to himself that would suit him to the ground. Of course, he would spend time in London. Probably go up during the season, because he knew the next thing would be Papa taking up the idea that his heir should wed and beget other heirs. He'd already played the invalid card, saying how frail he'd felt lately, and how he would love to see his grandchildren before completely losing his faculties.

'Nonsense,' Kit had said roundly. 'You might be confined to a chair but you make your presence known.'

'Ah well, you're young. How can I expect you to understand? At your age you think you have all the time in the world. But I'd like to see you make a suitable match.'

Kit wasn't too sure how he felt about that. He'd always had some romantic idea about marrying for love rather than convenience. Somehow he knew, he just knew, that his parents had had what was thought of as a love-match of a marriage. He could remember the two of them walking together hand-in-hand through the top meadow full of wildflowers and long grasses. He was usually racing ahead with one of the dogs, and occasionally, when he turned back, he'd see Pa's hand creep round his mother's waist and she would turn in the circle of his arm and reach up to kiss his cheek. He remembered feeling embarrassed at their soppiness at the same time as experiencing a warm feeling that his parents should like each other so much.

He supposed that was why he'd found it so hard to accept Arabella; he'd never seen her walk lazily in the top meadow hand-in-hand with Papa.

No, she was not his mother!

Kit heaved a heavy sigh. Perhaps he should allow Hugo a little leniency, make it clear to him that he wouldn't require the west wing until spring was underway. By then, Hugo might have become more reconciled to the idea of having Kit around, and more inclined to think of the gift of a house on the estate as something to be heartily pleased about. And, who knew, Arabella's charms might have lost a little of their appeal by then . . .

Deciding that a tactful talk with Hugo about his intentions might be his best course of action, and feeling the cold more than ever now he was on the east side of the building, he rounded the corner — and came close to bumping into a small upright figure wearing a pair of sturdy boots, a well-worn pelisse, and a shawl around her head which allowed just a few red-gold curls to escape before her ears.

'Georgie!' he exclaimed with pleasure.

Georgie failed to look so pleased. 'You should call me 'Miss Rankin',' she said disapprovingly.

'Yes, I should. Good morning Miss Rankin, and how are you on this bright sunny morn?'

She scowled. 'Cold! And wondering why on earth I agreed to come to Yorkshire in December.'

'Ah well, Jane informs me it was out of the goodness of your heart, and also because you couldn't resist the challenge of the portrait. And,' he added, peering more closely at her expression, 'I believe she has the right of it.'

'Well, your sister also believes that, although I'm not too old to be taking up challenges, I am a long-in-the-tooth spinster with a mysterious past.'

'She is misinformed, you are not yet twenty . . . ' He smiled. 'But do you have a mysterious past?'

'My past is boring and blameless.'

'Apart from when you masquerade as a boy?'

She glanced at him sharply. 'That was a necessity, as you know full well.'

A freezing blast of wintry air swept along the side of the building, causing Kit to gasp and Georgie to nearly lose her footing. Kit resisted the urge to take her arm. She looked so small and vulnerable against the monochrome landscape, and yet he knew she had an inner strength that could possibly rival his own. In order to shelter her a little, he moved closer but took care not to touch her.

'Tell me,' he asked, suddenly curious.

'How did you manage after your father was killed so suddenly?'

Georgie shot him a quick glance from under the shawl. 'I managed satisfactorily, thank you. There were paintings left that I could sell. Portraits I had to collect payments for.'

'Portraits to finish?'

'Assuredly,' she said curtly.

'And nobody questioned your work? Nobody noticed it was different from your father's?'

Georgie gave a half-laugh. 'By that time there was no difference. Most of it was my work. Anything long-distance he could hardly make out . . . I think that might have been the cause of his accident . . . ' Her voice trailed off.

'I see.' Keeping pace with her, he took a few more steps.

'I very much doubt it.'

'I've only seen your drawings. But to me at any rate, they looked extremely proficient.'

Georgie had no false modesty. 'Yes, they were . . . Extremely. Have you had occasion to study your own portrait?'

'I have. I thought your father did a good job.'

'Thank you, Mr Merryfield. You have answered your own question.'

He thought of Georgie sitting in her corner. The pages of noses, mouths, ears, and then full-length poses. 'Are you telling me that you did the majority of that study?'

Georgie shrugged. 'I asked his advice — he was good on uniforms. I made notes, colours, etcetera, but in the main — yes — I put it together. You were a good subject.'

He felt a stirring of admiration both for her talent and for her nerve. 'But you were only fifteen!'

Georgie nodded.

'Papa thinks highly of it.'

'I'm glad.'

'So the family portrait my father has commissioned from you will also be a success?'

'No reason why not. Unless, of course, you choose to inform on my duplicitous past.'

'You know me better than that.'

'On the contrary, I don't know you at all.'

They had reached the back door leading to the boot room. Kit turned to face her. Her small tip-tilted nose was pink at the end, her grey eyes bright with the cold, and her bottom lip looked so inviting that Kit was struggling to keep his eyes off it — and his mouth, come to that.

'I'd like to rectify that,' he said slowly. 'I really would . . . as a friend,' he went on, as he saw her involuntarily recoil.

He could see her start to open the door, and without thinking placed his hand, encased in a thick woollen glove, over hers — in a thinner, much-darned one.

'I'd very much like to ask you to do something for me,' he said.

Suspiciously, she met his eyes. 'And what might that be?'

'It's Papa,' he said. 'He won't have his portrait painted. Not since the accident. Wants to be remembered as he was in his prime. Understandable, I suppose . . . But I'd like something of him as he is now. And your drawings . . . well, I've a fancy you would get a true likeness, not necessarily a flattering likeness, but one of character . . . Well, could you do it from memory, d'you think?'

Georgie looked at him for a long time. 'I could,' she said at length. 'I could, but I won't. Not unless I have his permission.'

'Georgie — I mean, Miss Rankin — I'd be indebted to you if you would try to persuade him.'

★   ★   ★

It was all very well, thought Georgie, as she shook off her shawl and made her way up the back stairs to her room, it was all very well for Kit, walking back into her life in the way that he had and somehow coercing her into making rash promises that she had no hope of keeping. Why hadn't she just said no? *No, I can't do as you wish. I'm not here to dance to your tune.* Her original idea had been to execute a perfect family portrait, to have it admired by all the best people; and, incidentally, earn a place as a portrait painter specialising in mother and children groups. That was all!

It had all seemed so simple.

And now she was in a mess.

And there was nothing she hated more than mess!

She'd have to talk to the frightening Mr Joshua Merryfield, with all his harrumphing and his piercing glances, not to mention his fearsome eyebrows bristling away at her as though he knew very well all her business but was keeping quiet for reasons best known to himself.

He was one of the old school, and doubtless would consider it unthinkable that she, a mere woman, would have the temerity to even suggest she could sketch him.

But if he did agree . . . a small voice whispered in her ear. If he were to agree, what an accolade it would be: a man, a distinguished member of the gentry, agreeing to a pencil sketch being completed by a mere slip of a young female!

It would be an amazing breakthrough. Whether or not she would ever boast of it later, she wasn't sure, but *she* would know. That was the important thing.

Georgie had no doubts about her ability. Drawing was what she had been born to do. It was her first love from the age when she could very first hold a piece of charcoal in her small chubby fingers. And Joshua Merryfield would be a marvellous subject. A face full of character, full of experience; not all of it good. Already her fingers were itching in a way they simply did not when it came to painting the young and beautiful.

Oh yes, she knew she had to ask him — and not just because Kit had requested it of her, either. Although she had to admit to herself that when Kit looked at her a certain way, she was hard pushed to deny him.

All at once she felt excited. Excited and brave because, somewhere in the back of her mind, ever since the first time she'd met Joshua Merryfield — bristling eyebrows and all — she had almost pre-empted this moment!

The only problem was — when and how would she ask him?

6

By the time Jane, Lizzie and Josh arrived at the schoolroom, Georgie had already set up her equipment and was working from her earlier sketches.

'How can you work without us being here?' demanded Lizzie.

'That's why I make sketches. I'm working on blocking out the forms. I need you for checking and detailing, and also for establishing that the relationships I have between you are correct. That's very important in a group portrait.'

'Lizzie, you ask too many questions,' admonished Jane, obviously feeling uncomfortable with Lizzie's manner.

Ignoring her sister, Lizzie fixed insolent eyes on Georgie. 'I'd have thought our relationships obvious. We're the children, Mama's the mother.'

'I meant relationships in terms of

distances, negative spaces. And now I must concentrate — Jane will explain if you don't understand.'

'Mama is too busy to come this morning,' said Jane. 'She sends her apologies.'

Lizzie gave a snort of derision.

'Well, if you could just take your places as we discussed last time . . . No, Josh, please don't go near my paints, some of them are toxic! If you would just sit on the floor, Josh, where you were yesterday, that's it — perfect . . . I know you'll all want to get away as soon as possible in order to prepare for your visitors, so I'd like to get started right away.'

'We've only got this morning,' said Lizzie. 'When guests come, you know, we have to be ready to greet them.'

'Naturally,' said Georgie, beginning to take an active dislike to Lizzie.

'Mama said they won't be here until this afternoon at the earliest, but definitely before dark,' volunteered Jane. 'I can't wait. I can't wait to see

Prudence . . . and Charles,' she added, her face a little pink.

'Huh,' said Lizzie. 'He was covered in spots the last time.'

'His shirt points were high enough to take his eyeball out,' added Josh. 'And he kept saying *I say, that's capital!* and *By Jupiter!* all the time.'

'Oh, so that's where you got it from,' said Lizzie.

Georgie smiled. Sibling rivalry, family teasing. They were a normal family after all.

After an hour of work, Georgie felt the sort of excitement that told her things were beginning to come together. She stepped back and viewed her work critically. Yes, the preliminaries were showing promise that the portrait would be a good one.

'Take a ten-minute break,' she said. 'Stretch a bit and move around. I'd like you to pose for another hour if possible.'

Josh crept up behind her and looked aghast at what was on the easel.

'Doesn't look much at the moment, does it?' asked Georgie with a twitch of her lips. 'Don't worry, it never does at first.'

'Why do we have green faces?'

'Because that's what we call under-painting. Flesh tones contain all sorts of different hues. A good flesh tone can take layers of different glazes.'

'Oh,' said Josh.

'Fascinating,' said Lizzie in a bored voice.

Halfway through the next session, there was a tap on the door and Hugo walked in.

'Ah, here you are,' he said, rubbing his hands together for warmth. 'Weather's on the turn. It's freezing outside, but at least it's warm in here. Luncheon will be early, I was told to tell you. About another half-hour.'

He smiled around at them and came to look at the portrait.

'It looks awful at the moment,' said Josh conversationally. 'But don't worry about it. It's always like that at first,

Miss Rankin said so.'

'Then I'm sure she's right.'

Georgie laughed.

'I'll leave you to get on, then, and see you at luncheon.'

'You're very lucky,' said Lizzie when he'd gone.

'How so?' replied Georgie.

Lizzie looked up slyly from under her lashes. 'To take your meals with us.'

Georgie mixed some paint, this time with less thinner. 'I don't understand.'

'Well, usually the above-stairs servants eat together with the housekeeper and Miss Garvie.'

Jane coloured and gasped. 'Only in the London house,' she said quickly.

'I see.'

'So would you not agree?' went on Lizzie relentlessly. 'That you are lucky, to be treated as a member of our family here, when you are just a portrait painter?'

'Lizzie,' exclaimed her anguished sister. 'You go too far.'

'Well, it's only what Mama said.'

Georgie gave Lizzie a level look. She had been itching to put the precocious young Lizzie in her place. 'You know, it's a strange thing, but I find that the more I practise my skills, the luckier I become . . . Would you say luck alone enabled me to obtain a position at a prestigious academy for young ladies, or did proficiency have a hand in that?' She gave a smile of a sereneness she was far from feeling. 'In my experience, being tenacious and willing to learn are more reliable attributes than mere good fortune. Added to which, there is a certain satisfaction in the knowledge that once you have developed a skill, it cannot be taken from you. After all, fortune is a fickle thing. Who knows when it might be taken away?'

Lizzie opened her mouth, then closed it again.

'I've also learned,' went on Georgie, warming to her theme, 'that good manners are important too. Indeed, as Jane will tell you, at the academy we value good manners above all things.

Every pupil has to learn the difference between good and bad manners. We are judged on our manners no matter what station of life we are from.'

'Are you insinuating that my manners are bad?' asked Lizzie in a shaky voice.

Georgie turned an expression of the utmost blandness upon her. 'Did I say that?'

There was a short silence.

'I've had a capital idea. Would you make a drawing of my puppy?' asked Josh, totally oblivious to any undertones in the exchange that had just taken place. 'You could come to the stables and draw him then put him in the painting afterwards. Papa would like that, and I would too. Jane, do you think Mama would object if we did it like that?'

'Well, we'd have to ask. Likely it will be permitted, but it will be perishing cold out there.' said Jane.

'We'll see, then,' said Georgie, nettled that she'd allowed herself to be

159

provoked into almost open warfare with Lizzie, but grateful for the change in conversation. 'Perhaps there'll be time later.'

She worked on steadily until she judged it to be time for luncheon, when she dismissed the children before climbing on a chair to retrieve her pigment box from the top shelf. Ah yes, she did have enough white to start on the flesh tones and to cover the pastel shades of the girls' gowns. She locked the box again, got down from the chair, and returned the key to the pocket of her smock.

'Ah — alone, I see.'

Georgie looked up quickly as Hugo sidled in again. 'There'll be snow before too long,' he said, rubbing his hands together again and eyeing her in a way that made Georgie think he might be on the verge of taking a bite out of her. 'Heavy snow, too, by the look of the clouds building up. Are you nearly finished here? You are to come to luncheon too, you know.'

'So I understand.'

'It's an informal affair. Just some cold cuts, and a cheese or two.'

'Sounds most appetising.' Georgie turned to put her last brush, handle-downwards, in an earthenware pot. 'I'll come directly.'

'I'll escort you if I may?'

'Well, of course you may. I'd like to tidy myself first, however.'

Ogling her appreciatively, he took a step closer. 'You look delightful . . . But, might I add, you always do.'

Oh dear, there was no mistaking his tone. Hugo clearly thought a young semi-servant on the scene was fair game for a little flirting.

The look she gave him was not unlike the one she'd given Lizzie earlier — bland and unsmiling. She was just about to say 'Really?' in her most uninviting tone when the schoolroom door creaked open further.

'Ah, Hugo.' Kit's head appeared round the half-open door. 'Right, I was coming to find Miss Rankin to tell her luncheon is ready, but I see you have beaten me to it.'

'I'm just coming,' said Georgie, hurriedly drying her hands then smoothing them over her hair which was pinned back in a neat chignon.

'Perhaps you would go on, Hugo, and engage Arabella in conversation; she has arrived at table early, and won't take gladly to luncheon being delayed at all.'

After giving Kit a penetrating glance, Hugo complied and set off down the corridor.

Kit glanced at Georgie darkly. 'Is he making a nuisance of himself?'

Georgie almost laughed out loud. 'Now, why should that be the case?'

'Just a fancy of mine. Hugo's rather a ladies' man, but I happen to know he's frying his fish elsewhere.'

Georgie sniffed the air. 'No, only linseed oil. No trace of fish here, Mr Merryfield.'

'Beware those who smile too much. Hugo smiles a lot.'

'Yes, I'd noticed. It's so much more

attractive than a scowl.'

'I wasn't scowling.'

'Indeed not. It was only a passing comment ... Come on, then, we should make haste. Mrs Merryfield is anxious to start the meal on time, is she not?'

Scowling, as though to show he knew what a scowl really was, Kit moved away from the door to allow her to precede him. 'After we've eaten, it might be a good time to approach my father,' he said. 'He likes to retire to the library, and it's true he will often take a nap there; but he's been in good spirits this morning, doesn't seem tired, and I think the time is right. The girls and my stepmother will be making ready for the arrival of our guests, so you won't be able to work on the group portrait anyway.'

'You're determined this is a good notion?'

'Yes. I think if he allows anyone to draw him, it will be you. He's taken a fancy to you.'

'Now, how can you know that?'

'He was fond of your father, and I can tell he likes what he's seen of you. I think now would be a good time.'

She turned to face him and found herself looking straight up into his dark eyes. They were the sort of eyes that could make you forget every resolve you had ever made about non-involvement with clients. Eager to break their spell, she blinked 'You understand that if he refuses, that will be an end of it?'

They were holding one another's gaze for longer than was appropriate. His eyes were warm and dark, and still it was impossible for her to look away.

'I understand,' he said at last. He lifted his hand and touched the side of her nose with his forefinger. 'Forgive me; you had a smear of green paint on your nose.'

'Thank you,' she said, her heart beating wildly as, at a sedate pace suitable to a teacher of young ladies who would firmly rebuff any thoughts of romance with the heir of the household, she followed said heir down the corridor.

* * *

True to Kit's word, it was to the library that Joshua Merryfield repaired when luncheon was over.

Georgie hovered outside. She could hear the log fire spitting and cracking within. Hesitating on the threshold, she peered round the door and, seeing him sitting in his chair staring at the flames, ventured a few steps forward. The old grizzled lurcher at his feet lifted an ear and opened one eye.

'Come in if you're coming, I don't bite! And neither does Grey.'

Trying not to feel intimidated, Georgie tiptoed a little further. She had her sketching book under her arm, and a cloth bag containing pencils and sepia chalks over her wrist.

'Are you very busy, sir?'

From beneath the beetling brows a pair of sharp dark eyes scrutinized her.

165

'Do I look busy? I wish I were. No, I'm just a useless old man, and nothing makes me more aware of it than seeing a young miss like you creeping about, afraid she might disturb me.'

'I wasn't *creeping about*,' said Georgie hotly. 'I was looking to ask if I might draw you.'

The bright eyes regarded her for some moments as though trying to decide whether to beetle some more, or admit defeat. 'No, you might not,' he said eventually. 'Why should you want to? There are no reasons to draw me.'

'There are two very good reasons, sir.'

His eyebrows went up. 'Two, eh? And what might those be?'

'First, I have wanted to draw you ever since I first saw you. Your face is interesting, your features strong . . . your expression . . . ' She caught his eye. ' . . . terrifying, actually!'

There was a short bark of laughter. 'Terrifying, eh? Well, what's the other reason?'

'Guessing what your answer to such a request would be, your son Kit asked me to draw you from memory . . . I said I would rather ask you first.'

'Did he now?' His expression softened. 'I wonder why?'

'You need hardly ask that, sir. It's obvious that he thinks very highly of you.'

Mr Merryfield shifted in his chair wincing with pain as he did so. 'Harrumph! Think highly of him too . . . of course I do. Proud of him. Proud of all my children. But Kit, firstborn you know, turned out to be a fine young man. Could have been different. Could have been a wastrel.'

Georgie drew a breath. It was time to press home her advantage. 'So you'll agree to my sketching you?'

'Hmm. When d'you intend to start, then?'

'Now, if you like. There's no time like the present.'

'Harrumph! We have guests arriving today.'

'So I believe ... A few pencil or chalk sketches won't take long. I only ask that you sit comfortably with your head turned towards the light.'

'I'm never comfortable.'

Georgie sat down opposite him and set her sketching block on her lap. 'Surely more so now, since your son is home and no longer fighting on foreign soil?'

'Indeed.' His gaze relaxed and for a few moments he stared ahead, seemingly lost in a world of thought. Tentatively, Georgie started to make a few marks on her paper.

A sudden sigh escaped her subject. 'Although, I feel now I can die happy.'

Georgie looked up. 'Not immediately, I hope? I should like to produce at least one worthwhile likeness of you.'

He gave a deep chuckle. 'I expect you would . . . No, it's not much of a life for the active man I used to be. I've borne it, in the main for the sake of my family. Don't want to put a gun to my head. Messy business. Besides, damned bad form. Don't want to drag on, either. Maybe just long enough to see Kit take up the reins again . . . I've a good feeling about that. Like his mother, strong . . .

'Mad as hell when I married Arabella. I tried to explain she was never a replacement for his Mama . . . Arabella — flighty, flirtatious — entertaining. His own mother — more serious, reflective, romantic nature, totally unselfish.' He gave a tired smile. 'Two more different women you couldn't hope to find . . . I thought that would make it more acceptable . . . I was wrong.'

For a while there was peace in the room, except for the logs stirring and settling in the hearth, and the scratching of Georgie's charcoal. She sketched on, the planes of Joshua's face taking shape beneath her fingers. The firm line of his mouth, the hollows round his eyes, the haughtiness of his stare softened a little by fine lines of humour, and of pain, etched at the corners.

She was absorbed and happy, hardly listening to his words when he started to speak again, until she became suddenly aware that he'd asked her a question.

'Beg pardon. I was concentrating on my drawing, I didn't hear,' she faltered.

For a long moment, he stared at her. 'Hmm, just as well, probably,' he said. 'Just an old man's ruminations.'

'You're not old,' said Georgiana. 'Not that old, anyway.'

Again that bark of amusement. 'Not in the head,' he said. 'And that's the torment.'

Thinking of her own dear Pa, Georgie sighed 'Your son is home. This is surely not the time to be sorry for . . . ' She stopped short, aware that she might be overstepping the mark.

'Go on. You were going to say 'sorry for yourself', weren't you? Well, you're right young lady, I'll stop being so blue-devilled. I'll welcome my guests to my house, watch my wife glowing in her role as hostess, her cousin with an irritating smirk ever-present, young Lizzie as precocious as ever, Jane and Josh their ever-sweet selves, and of course — Kit — my returned son and heir; and I'll rejoice that we are all together under my roof and about to celebrate Christmas ... ' He leaned forward in his chair, and as he did so a spasm of discomfort crossed his features. 'There, that enough for you?'

Recognising fear as well as suffering in his eyes, Georgie regarded him steadily. Somehow the beetling brows weren't so frightening any more. 'I would appreciate another sitting,' she said calmly. 'But I have enough for now.' She didn't refer to the fact that it was obvious he had also had enough. She had discovered sufficient about him to know that he was a proud man.

Proud and in pain.

'Thank you for your patience, sir,' she said collecting her pencils together. 'I'll leave you in peace now.'

'I knew your mother,' he said suddenly.

In the act of standing, Georgiana froze. 'Did you?'

'Oh yes ... You're like her, too. Remarkable woman. Gave up everything in order to be with your father, and he was a rascally fellow.'

Georgie opened her mouth to remonstrate.

'Good artist, but only a second son.' He shrugged his shoulders. 'No money, of course.'

Georgie laughed. 'Oh, I know,' she said feelingly.

'Your mother came from good lineage. The Langleys.'

Reluctant to continue the conversation, Georgie straightened and picked up her sketchbook. 'So I believe,' she said shortly. 'I have no contact with them. Nor would I want any.'

Joshua Middleton chuckled. 'Got your father's spirit as well as his hair. You'll do!'

Do for what exactly, she wasn't quite sure. With a slight nod of the head she left the library.

* ⋆ ★

The schoolroom door was ajar. That was the first thing Kit noticed, with annoyance, because the schoolroom faced north and was therefore cold even on the warmest of days. The second thing he noticed, this time with disappointment, was that it was empty. He paused on the threshold. It was nearly an hour since luncheon, and he'd hoped Georgie would be back by now. But on the one hand, that was good, because it meant that they were getting along — and somehow it was important to him that Georgie and Papa dealt well together. But, on the other hand, it meant that he'd have to wait longer before seeing her again; and somehow seeing her again — in fact, seeing her as much as possible — had also become very important to him.

Oh well, he'd just have to be patient for a little longer. She'd said she was planning to come back to the school-room to continue working on the background of the portrait. Kit went on into the schoolroom, and frowned at the fireplace where a smouldering mass of grey ash lurked. Obviously no one had thought to make up the fire since lunch. He looked around. The collection of logs piled to one side of the hearth did not include kindling. His shoulder was stiff rather than painful now. This was a good sign, because it meant that, despite the horrendous carriage journey, his wound was healing. But he had the use of one good arm, his wounded arm from the elbow down, and both of his hands. He wondered if he'd be able to get a decent fire burning by the time she arrived.

Using his good shoulder to support himself, he knelt in front of the fire and stirred the embers. Good, there were a few sparks left. He selected the smallest and driest of the logs, strategically placing it on the faintly glowing embers, then looked round for something to draw the flames. He was in luck. There, standing to the side of the hearth — but annoyingly just out of reach — was a sheet of metal obviously intended for that very purpose. Surely he could reach that far without hurting his damn shoulder. Balancing on the balls of his feet, he leaned to one side.

Good, he'd managed to grasp the metal sheet, but it proved heavier than he'd thought. Slowly he dragged it towards him.

There was the sound of light footsteps in the corridor, a door opening, then a sharp intake of breath.

'Goodness, you made me jump! What on earth are you doing down there?'

Kit turned his head. It was her. He gave a delighted smile, which turned to a cry of anguished embarrassment as he slowly toppled over. The next instant he was staring at the ceiling, recognising the same cracks that had been there for as long as he could remember, then there was an anxious but beautiful upside-down face above him.

'Oh dear, it's the second time in two

days I've managed to knock you over! Are you alright? Where does it hurt? Should I fetch someone?'

Briefly, he shut his eyes. What a clumsy buffoon he must appear. 'Yes, I'm perfectly alright; only my sensibilities are in any way hurt; and no, most definitely — do not fetch anyone.'

'But what were you doing?' asked Georgie, looking as though she were trying hard not to smile.

'I was trying to get the fire going.'

'I can do that in a moment. I'd have thought you'd summon someone to attend to it for you.'

'I can do things for myself, thank you,' said Kit, struggling to sit up.

Seeming to deem it wisest not to argue, Georgie put out a hand and pulled him to a sitting position. 'Here let me help!'

Actually, her hand in his felt good. Thirty seconds later, his hand was still holding hers and it still felt good.

'You look pale. You won't faint, will you?'

'Only ladies faint. I'm made of sterner stuff.'

'Of course you are!' said Georgie robustly. 'Now, if I bring a chair over and help a bit, do you think you'd be able to get on it?'

'I can try.'

'Well, if so, I'd quite like my hand back.'

Reluctantly, he complied. 'Of course; stupid of me. Apologies. You must think I'm a complete dolt.'

His hand now felt strangely bereft.

The smile became a reality. She looked lovely when she smiled.

'Well, a little foolish, perhaps. Now, if you're up to it, I think perhaps you should try for the chair.'

Kit watched as she dragged over one of the schoolroom chairs, then he found that by taking his weight mainly on his legs and using his good arm to steady himself, it wasn't too difficult to haul himself up from floor level. No, it wasn't difficult, but the exercise became altogether more pleasurable with Georgie's arm round his waist, her hair just tickling the underside of his chin, the fresh lemon scent of it in his nostrils.

'We did it,' she said triumphantly as he managed to perch on the wooden seat.

Kit, whose eyes were now level with Georgie's elegant throat, was having problems breathing. 'Thank you,' he said eventually.

'Glad to oblige.' Her eyes crinkled with amusement. 'Just think, if I hadn't happened along, you might have been stuck on the floor for hours!'

He could see a pulse beating in her slim neck. 'That would have been very droll, I'm sure.'

'So, I'd better see to this fire.' She bent her head, and suddenly her cheek was very close to his. He only had to lift his head a little, turn it like so, have time to take in the wide look of surprise and — oh joy — surrender in her eyes, and before he knew it he was tasting that delicious bottom lip of his dreams, feeling the strength and the softness of her small body close to his.

With his good arm he pulled her closer. 'Georgie,' he said into the lemon-scented hair just above her ear, 'I've wanted to do that for so long.'

But, with a look of horror on her face, Georgie was pushing him away. 'No,' she said. 'That wasn't meant to happen. Should never have happened. I must go. I'm sorry. Forgive me. I must go!'

And she'd gone!

Kit was left feeling sad and bewildered, then furious with himself for bungling the situation, then secretly pleased because before she'd realised what was happening, before reality had stepped in, Georgie had responded. Her mouth had been soft, receptive, and eager for his kiss.

Kit, he told himself, *you are in with a chance. Your case is not lost.* Not won yet either, it was true, but Kit was an experienced campaigner.

He glanced out of the window. Snow

was falling; Georgiana was going nowhere soon.

After a moment's contemplation, he decided there was no point in continuing to nurse the feeble smoulderings in the grate. Clearly Georgie would take time to compose herself, and would in all probability stay in her room until she absolutely had to come out, which wouldn't be until it was time to dine.

Wincing, he rose from the old wooden chair. He intended to make his way back to the library, look in to see if Papa was there napping, and if he was, sneak in there unnoticed and take possession of a comfortable armchair. He wouldn't be needed until the visitors arrived, and then only to put in a desultory appearance, do the pretty, and retire again to the fireside while the guests were settled. Later, of course, when Doctor Bainbridge and his wife arrived, he would want to pass some time with him discussing Papa's health.

This decided, Kit left the schoolroom and, with his shoulders back in true soldier fashion, strode down the corridor.

He was surprised to find Lizzie lurking in the shadows by the stairs.

'Hello Lizzie, you're looking pretty. Is that a new gown?'

Lizzie went a little pink. 'Yes. Mama said I might change early because I won't be at dinner tonight; I can have tea with the guests but have to have supper with Josh. I'm not old enough to attend dinner, you see,' she added bitterly.

'Well, you won't be missing very much,' said Kit sympathetically. 'If I could tell you about the number of boring dinners I've had to sit through, you wouldn't be so eager to experience them. There'll be a lot of talk about gout and what this person said to that person at the last social gathering. It won't be very entertaining.'

Lizzie stuck out her lower lip. 'Yes, but there will be jokes and talk of dresses and dances ... It's only because of Josh. I'm sure Mama would let me attend dinner if it weren't for him. I have to bear company with him all the time. He's a *boy*!'

'Yes, I'd noticed. Cheer up, Lizzie, I know it must be a sore trial for you to be neither the youngest nor the oldest. I can remember being your age; it wasn't a very good time for me either. I had to eat in the nursery with my two younger sisters and a *baby*.'

Lizzie looked at him with begrudging respect. 'Yes, of course. I'd nearly forgotten. But you didn't have to do so for long. At least you were able to go to school, and it was only in the holidays.'

There seemed no answer to that.

'The snow's settling,' he said, for something to say. 'You'll be able to get the old sledge out. I'll wager Prudence and Charles won't think themselves too grown-up to go sledging. You can all go out tomorrow. It'll be a great lark!'

Her face brightened. Then a sly look came over it. 'What about Miss Rankin? If she's not painting us, d'you think she'll come too?'

Kit, who had been hoping for a rendezvous with Georgie at some time tomorrow, and knowing that tobogganing for him was out of the question, tried not to look despondent. 'You'd have to ask her. But of course, she's not used to the country; she might prefer to remain inside.'

Lizzie arched an eyebrow in a way that put Kit in mind of Arabella. 'Well, you could keep her company. I daresay she wouldn't be bored then!'

Kit gave her a searching glance. Now, why would she say that, and in just such a manner?

Giving a short laugh over his shoulder, he turned on his way.

Some time later, after a conversation with his father mainly regarding matters of the management of the estate, Kit, who had drifted off into a pleasant state of being not quite asleep but not quite awake either, was aware of sounds of arrivals.

Faint snores were issuing forth from behind the wing of Papa's chair.

Fearing one of the children might burst in and disturb him, Kit hauled himself to his feet and went along to the stairs which led to the great hall.

Despite its name, the great hall was by no means great. It was the hall where callers were received, and was considerably larger than the original hall of the house, which was now used by the estate workers on their way to the estate office in the west wing.

He arrived at the top of the stairs to find that the visitors had stamped the snow from their boots and had their outer garments taken by Brewer. Overnight luggage was standing to the side, waiting to be taken to the guest rooms. Arabella was already greeting the family in a warm fashion, and Kit was just in time to witness a breathless Jane arrive on the scene, pulling a reluctant Georgiana by the hand.

'I just can't wait to introduce you to Prudence,' Jane was saying. 'I've told her so much about you, and Prudence just loves to paint in watercolours. And

oh, yes — ' She went even pinker.
' — this is Prudence's brother,
Charles . . . '

'Slow down,' Georgie was saying.
'Please wait a moment, Jane, give your
friends a moment to compose themselves.'

Prudence's father turned, and Kit
recognised him directly as being an old
friend of his own Papa's. Immediately
he descended the staircase with his
hand outstretched in greeting. 'Squire
Ashton,' he said. 'How very good it is to
see you again. Kit Merryfield at your
service.' As the two men shook hands,
Kit looked over the older man's
shoulder, and took in Georgiana's
expression of dismay.

In a moment, the expression was
gone to be replaced with one of slight
but professional interest. Squire Ashton
had by this time wheeled round and
was regarding her through sharp eyes.
'But I know you, don't I?' he said
directly to Georgie. 'We've met before.
Never forget a face, do I, Mrs Ashton?'

Mrs Ashton, a small lady with a round obliging face, nodded in agreement. 'No, no, he never does.'

Georgie gave a light laugh. 'Well, it's no wonder you think so. My Pa painted your portrait once, so I believe.'

'Of course,' said Arabella easily. 'It was Squire Ashton who convinced us to engage your father to paint the portrait of Kit before he went off to soldier for the King. And now this is his daughter, who may not be quite so proficient as her Papa, but is still much sought-after as a portrait painter of children. She is engaged to paint a group portrait of me and the young ones.'

Squire Ashton was still staring at Georgie with puzzlement in his eyes. 'No, it's you I remember,' he said.

'Unfortunately, my father and my brother have both passed away,' said Georgie, her voice rivalling Arabella's for smoothness. 'I was used to keep house for them, you know, and only painted for pleasure. Alas, now they are both gone . . . Did you ever come to our studio, sir? I don't have a memory of it, but maybe . . . '

It was no good. Kit couldn't continue to watch her struggle. 'Oh, well, that would be it! Your brother — of course! He was your father's, apprentice wasn't he? And looked very much like you, I seem to remember?'

'Maybe,' said Squire Ashton. 'Scrawny lad? I remember him. Name of Georgie, I believe.'

'No,' said Georgie. 'His name was Tommy. My name is Georgiana, but Pa often called me Georgie, and sometimes he got the names confused.'

'Well, anyway,' said Arabella, clearly not pleased at the limelight being all on Georgiana, 'you must come to the drawing room and warm up. My husband is at the moment resting in the library, but I will send Lizzie to fetch him directly and we may all be cosy together.' She turned her eyes towards Georgie. 'Now, I know Miss Rankin has some rather pressing work to attend to, so she will have to desert us, I'm afraid;

but we will all meet up for dinner. We're expecting Doctor and Mrs Bainbridge, and also the Reverend Richardson, to join us . . . '

Kit watched as the party were slowly led upstairs; Mrs Ashton to be shown straight to her room, the squire to be refreshed with a small glass of brandy. Kit felt he could do with one himself. Soon the hall was deserted, apart from Brewer who was fussing over the luggage, and Georgie and Kit who were left staring at one another, the space between them feeling far too wide.

Thank you, mouthed Georgie silently.

I love you, Kit mouthed back before following the others. At the turn of the stairs he looked back to smile.

But Georgie had gone.

7

With her heart, mind, body and soul in turmoil, Georgiana scuttled down the nearest corridor. Her customary façade of calm had quite deserted her and all she wanted to do was escape,.

What was she *doing*?

What was *he* thinking?

She'd no sooner recovered from his kiss — the kiss that had turned out to be *their* kiss, sweet and gentle, tender and sensitive — everything she'd always known a kiss should be; she'd just calmed herself, or nearly so, and then, on the heels of being confronted by Squire Ashton, who she'd always known to be clever and calculating: wallop! Kit had stepped in and saved her — again! And then had the audacity to mouth to her that he loved her!

I love you, his lips had said

Of course, he didn't mean it.

Couldn't mean it. He wanted a small flirtation, that was all. Along with Hugo, he wanted something to pass away the hours in this Godforsaken, cold, murky place called Yorkshire. A place where the brooding hills looked satanic, and the rivers ran exceeding cold — what else was there to do?

She gave a shiver and, pretending she'd never seen him mouth those words, straightened her posture and forced herself to stop scuttling like a frightened mouse. Somehow she had to carry on.

A small staircase, that Georgie recognised as being the one that Jane had dragged her down only a little while ago, was at the end of the corridor. Hoping that a servant wouldn't disturb her, she shakily sat down on the bottom step. For a moment she was furious with Pa, who had been the one to suggest her masquerading as a boy in the first place. Then she forced herself to think rationally and in the present. She had always been destined to meet the Ashtons at some stage, she supposed, so at least that trial was over.

After a few more contemplative moments, she wended her way back through the maze of corridors until she found herself outside the schoolroom.

She could hear china chinking against a background of Miss Garvie's fluttering voice admonishing Josh for cramming his mouth too full. That meant that neither Kit nor Hugo were present. Georgie had noticed that Miss Garvie rarely spoke if either man were in the vicinity. A wise woman indeed. Georgie resolved to try to emulate Miss Garvie's modest behaviour in future.

Sure enough, only the governess and Josh were present. As things stood, she couldn't imagine she would have another sitting with Arabella or Jane until the guests had gone, but she might catch an hour or two with Lizzie and Josh. She wondered exactly how long the guests were staying. 'A few days,' Jane had said. 'They'll be gone by

Christmas Day.' A few days of avoiding Squire and Mrs Ashton's company, avoiding prying questions about 'Tommy', as well as side-stepping Kit, with his ridiculous notions about a dalliance with the art teacher!

I love you.

It was a joke. It must be a joke. Her eyes sparked. How dare he make a joke at her expense!

It took extreme concentration to make sense of what Miss Garvie was saying.

'Please join us, Miss Rankin.' It sounded more of an entreaty than an invitation. Miss Garvie was obviously desperate for adult company.

Georgie's eyes swept over the table. The two of them were partaking of an afternoon tea which was heavy on crumpets and cakes and low on boring sandwiches. The curtains were drawn against the snowy outdoors; there was now a hearty fire in the grate, and a toasting fork resting against the fender. The room looked invitingly cosy.

'The girls are to have tea with the guests, who've arrived just at the right time,' explained Josh out of a mouth full of cake. 'Which means — all the more for me, of course! I pretended I was upset to be left out, so Mama gave instructions to make my tea rather special. Would you like to toast a crumpet? It's the most fun, especially if it catches alight — once I made Lizzie scream and burnt the rug. You can still see the mark.'

'Thank you,' Georgie murmured, thinking she really couldn't eat a thing and probably never would again. 'It looks delicious, but I'm expected to eat dinner tonight.' From the corner of her eye she saw Mis Garvie's face fall. 'Though I must admit, a cup of tea would be most refreshing,' she added swiftly.

Amidst much fluttering, tea was poured into a cup of fine bone china and passed to Georgie, who took a sip and sighed appreciatively.

'That's lovely . . . Thank you, Miss

Garvie. Um, will you be at dinner tonight?' she asked, struggling to be sociable.

'I've been invited to attend, yes, and I'm sure it will be most enjoyable,' said Miss Garvie in an anxious tone which indicated quite the opposite sentiment.

'It must be awkward, never knowing which meals you are to attend and which not.'

The governess sighed. 'When the girls are asked to sing, my piano playing sometimes proves useful. Do you play, Miss Rankin?'

'Sadly not. I fear my usefulness is limited.'

Miss Garvie patted her hair. 'Occasionally, although I'm not proficient, I'm asked to make up a hand at cards; it's all very convivial, I'm sure.'

'I'm sure,' echoed Georgie, who had by now a fair idea that poor Miss Garvie could be summoned at any time of the day or night with no thought to her own feelings in the matter. 'My card playing isn't up to scratch, but I can just about manage chequers.'

'When will you come to see my new puppy?' asked Josh, obviously bored with this polite ladies' talk.

'When the weather warms up a bit. It's far too cold at the moment.'

'It's warm in the stables. The horses give off a tremendous amount of heat, and anyway, Floss that's the mother — she's found a corner and made a nest of hay.'

'Have you decided what to call him yet?'

'I thought maybe Ripper, because he ripped at my jacket with his teeth, but Jem said he didn't think much of that.'

'Jem?'

'He's my friend. He's a stable lad. Don't tell Mama, though, she thinks stable lads are a bad influence.'

'And are they?'

'Probably,' said Josh with a grin. 'But I don't care for that. I like him, and he knows all the best places to fish, the best trees to climb, and the best dogs for ratting.'

Miss Garvie gave a refined shudder, so Georgie didn't comment that she could have done with a good ratter in the London studio six months ago. 'I see,' she said instead.

'He's sort of bouncy,' went on Josh halfway through another cake. 'I mean the puppy, not Jem.'

'Well, call him Bouncer, then.'

'Bouncer! Yes, a capital idea ... Bouncer!'

After, at the same time as struggling to put all thoughts of Kit out of her mind, exchanging more pleasantries with Miss Garvie which even to her own ears sounded as dull as ditchwater, Georgie found herself pretending an interest in the many qualities Josh was looking for in his new pony. Finding that because she knew nothing about horses — or ponies, for that matter — she had nothing more to contribute, Georgie finished her tea and, after a smiling thank-you, left pleading a slight headache which by now was showing signs of being all too real.

Kit spent half an hour or so doing the pretty and sipping brandy with his father, Squire Ashton, and Hugo, who had arrived on the scene as though by accident. His surprise at finding them all together in the drawing room seemed to Kit to be a little contrived. He rather suspected that Hugo could never bear to be out of the know. Arabella, who was also present, positively glowed at having so many of the male species to entertain. Kit kept up his part of the conversation well, he thought, under the circumstances.

The circumstances being that he had suddenly realised that he was head over heels in love with Georgiana Rankin!

How it had happened, he didn't know. Quite *when* it had happened was another puzzling thing. Unexpectedly it had become, with surprising clarity, a sudden unalterable fact. Why the surprise? Despite their brief acquaintance, he knew her through and through. He knew she was brave, trustworthy, talented, straightforward — except for the invention of a brother, of course, and that had been more to do with her Papa than her. He knew the line of her cheek; the direction of the curl that escaped onto her neck; the clouds that, when she felt sad, sometimes appeared in her otherwise clear grey eyes; and now he also knew the taste of her sweet mouth, the softness of her small strong body, and the way that it could momentarily melt against his. Had Kit been of poetic inclination, he would have set about composing an ode directly. As it was, he smiled — indeed, it was difficult to keep the smile from his face. He made polite conversation about the snow that was piling up outside, about how Charles and Prudence had grown, about the coming Christmas festivities of a ball to be held in Harrogate, several card parties and country dances at neighbouring estates.

Just as Mrs Ashton and the younger members of the party arrived to partake of afternoon tea, he excused himself, appropriating a couple of sandwiches and a macaroon from a tray-carrying footman on his way out. 'Good job. Well done,' he said.

He looked in at the schoolroom to discover that, mentioning a headache and the need to rest in her room, Georgie had just left. In his turn, he too was entreated to partake of some tea, so took the opportunity to wolf down a couple more sandwiches and a cake. Miss Garvie fluttered and Josh told him a joke about the newest book out by a comrade of Wellington's. 'It's called *Forty Years in the Saddle* and it's by Major Bumsore,' he said, barely able to choke the words out with the effort of keeping a straight face.

Blushing scarlet, Miss Garvie reproved him.

Josh cast her a withering look. 'All right then, I beg pardon,' he said. 'But I daresay Kit must've heard ruder jokes than that! There's one about an actress and a bishop which I didn't quite understand, but Jem thinks no end funny.'

'All right Josh, that will do,' said Kit.

Unabashed Josh tucked into another piece of shortbread. 'Well, I don't see why we always have to be so starchy.'

His brother declined to comment, and after promising to come and see the new puppies in the stable on the morrow, said he must go now and rest up a bit before dinner.

'Miss Rankin might come to see Bouncer too,' said Josh. 'She thought to call him Bouncer. She's a good sort when she's not painting.'

'I'll look forward to it.'

After leaving the schoolroom, Kit toyed with the idea of visiting Georgie's room. Then common sense prevailed.

In true soldierly style, he straightened his shoulders; wincing a little as the wound, which was healing nicely, tightened. Come to think of it, he was feeling a little weary. He'd been told to get plenty of rest. Perhaps a nap before dinner wouldn't be out of the question.

He could lie down quietly in his room and think about Georgie.

Georgie's face, Georgie's eyes, Georgie's rare smile . . .

Later, revived by the longer-than-planned-for nap, Kit hummed to himself as, with his man Jenkins' help, he arranged his neck-cloth.

'Happy tonight, sir?' queried Jenkins.

'It's nice to be back with one's family again, Jenkins.'

'Indeed, sir, indeed,' replied Jenkins, whose puckered mouth told Kit he was privately deliberating on why the neck-cloth had to be tied with quite such precision.

But Kit, who had never been one to care too much for his appearance, suddenly wanted to appear to his best advantage. His evening attire verged on the conservative side, but the well-cut navy-blue coat and yellow pantaloons showed off his military figure. His dark hair, treated to the veriest trace of pomade, shone as he carefully arranged it.

After removing a minute fleck of dust from his lapel, he took a final glance at his reflection and thought he would stroll to the drawing room to await the announcement of dinner. He was early, but that was no matter; he could watch for Georgie's entrance and not miss a moment of her presence.

As he'd anticipated, the drawing room was empty, or nearly so. Arabella was standing with her back to him, oblivious to his entrance and clearly deep in thought. She looked beautiful — but then she always did, he thought dispassionately.

He cleared his throat and watched her expression change as she registered another presence, from contemplation to that of a vivacious, charming hostess. Her eyes hardened a little as she realised it was Kit disturbing her reverie.

'Ah, how fortuitous. I was wishing to speak with you.'

'At your service, ma'am,' Kit had never been able to form his lips round the word *Mama* when addressing her.

'Lizzie came to me today in a state of some agitation.'

Unable to imagine what was coming next Kit waited enquiringly.

'It seems she was unfortunate enough to witness a rather unedifying scene.' She paused for a moment. 'She is a young girl and highly impressionable,' she continued, turning to face him squarely.

Kit said nothing.

'Earlier this afternoon, she went to the schoolroom, believing that Miss Rankin would be there and requiring her to sit for the portrait. It seems she met with a distressing state of affairs . . . Now, I don't know exactly what you were about, Kit . . . '

There was a silence which Kit was reluctant to break. Arabella continued to look at him as though he had just crawled out from under a stone.

'Well, I don't know what it was that Lizzie saw, or thought she saw . . . ' he said eventually, hoping that the memory of that so-perfect kiss would not be forever sullied by the thought of Lizzie's observation.

'Oh, come now Kit, please grant me a little nous.' She gave a tinkling laugh. 'Really, I am quite broad-minded, and know well a young man's appetites — but under your father's roof?' Her eyebrows rose. 'And with someone who is little more than a servant?' Her eyebrows rose a notch higher.

A wave of anger overtook Kit, but he continued to stand motionless. 'Well, madam, I should think you would desist from admonishing me on that particular issue.'

Arabella's features sharpened, an almost imperceptible flicker of fear showing in the depth of her blue eyes. 'What can you mean?'

Kit treated her to one of his most haughty stares. 'You know well what I mean — but I'll say no more on that score. As for Lizzie, possibly she reads too many romantic novels. It seems she has put an inaccurate interpretation on my losing balance whilst attempting to relight the fire in the schoolroom. Fortunately, Miss Rankin happened along, and was able to help me up and assist me to the nearest chair. Unfortunately, my wound still pains me, and I was feeling a little dizzy . . . ' He put his hand to his shoulder to emphasize the point. 'I was glad of her shoulder to lean on . . . Meanwhile, I should like to remind you that Miss Rankin is here at my father's invitation, she is a highly respectable and intelligent young lady, and should be extended every courtesy. I trust I have made myself clear?'

'Lizzie doesn't lie, Kit!'

Kit bowed his head. 'No more do I, madam!'

Arabella turned away. 'I believe I hear the Reverend Richardson arriving,' she said into a silence that made it obvious she heard no such thing. 'Excuse me, I must greet my guests. Oh, and you will oblige me, Kit, by escorting Mrs Ashton in to dinner.'

She swept from the room.

Kit let out an expulsion of breath. Why was nothing ever simple? He wanted it to be. He wanted everything to be perfect, but he had to be realistic. He should watch his step, not behave like a lovesick swain, sighing with yearning and never tearing his eyes from his beloved's face. No, he must behave with decorum, with subtlety, or he might jeopardize Georgie's position in the household. No more seeking her out, no more gazing at her, no more snatched conversations — or kisses.

He caught himself on a groan. How was he supposed to make her love him, how was he meant to do his courting?

Maybe fifteen minutes later, the Reverend Richardson did indeed arrive and was ushered into the room. On seeing Kit, he extended a warm hand. 'My word,' he said. 'I had no idea you were back. Your father must be delighted.'

Kit got to his feet and was quickly engaged in conversation about the village, the estate and Reverend Richardson's parishioners.

By the time the other diners, including Doctor and Mrs Bainbridge and the Ashtons, had arrived, Kit had barely had the opportunity to glance up in order to notice Miss Garvie and Georgie enter. When he did in fact, snatch a quick look round, he discovered that Georgie — dressed in an unobtrusive, but again well-fitting, gown of dull olive — was deep in discussion with his father. She had seated herself on a low chair to be on a level with him, and Kit was surprised to see how easily they were conversing together. Papa's lips were twitching at something she'd just said, and Georgie was waiting enquiringly for some witty return. Eventually, he answered her; obviously a short answer, and a somewhat cheeky one, for Georgie coloured slightly as she struggled not to laugh too loudly.

'The little art teacher appears to have ingratiated herself with your father?'

It was a smiling Hugo. It would be of course!

'What's that Hugo? I was just thinking how well Papa is looking. The socialising appears to do him good.' Kit turned to Doctor Bainbridge. 'Would you not agree Doctor?'

'Certainly,' replied the doctor obligingly. 'Although I would have a notion it's more to do with your homecoming than anything else on the matter.'

Hugo agreed with a simper and then at a signal from Arabella went over to her, no doubt to be told who to lead in to the dinner table.

'All the same,' said Doctor Bainbridge, watching him go 'I should appreciate the opportunity, later, to speak to you regarding your father's health.'

Kit looked at him sharply. 'Yes, I will certainly make sure of that. I must confess myself to be a little anxious. Well, more than a little . . . He seems so frail, and although he makes no complaint, his breathing is laboured.'

The doctor laid a hand on Kit's cuff. 'He's looked after very well. Don't worry on that score. Arabella is good for him, and the children, of course. But he grows weary of his body not being able to do what he requires of it, and there have been times when his spirit is not quite what I would like. But — ' He looked towards where the diners were making their way towards the dining room. ' — we'll have a chance to talk further later.'

'Indeed we will,' replied Kit, preparing to cross the room to escort Mrs Ashton in to dinner as previously instructed.

Fortunately — or, then again, *unfor*tunately, thought Kit — he was seated at the other end of the table to Georgie. This was good in that he could look at her without appearing to do so, but bad in that he had no chance of conversing with her.

Her hair looked particularly lovely tonight, he noticed. It had been dressed in a looser knot at the back of her head, but a few curls were draped over her shoulder. The elegance of her creamy neck and the neat pearl necklace at her throat drew his attention to the hint of a modest cleavage. She looked every inch a lady.

The dinner party went on at a leisurely pace. Kit strived to keep his impatience under control. At the far end of the table, well away from Squire Ashton, he could see that Georgie ate a little of everything put before her and managed a restrained conversation with Doctor Bainbridge. Papa, when he wasn't listening to his guests, looked tired but benign. Arabella, in her role as hostess, was as vivacious as always, Hugo smiled his relentless smile; Jane and Prudence started to giggle; the reverend conversed together with Squire and Mrs Ashton about Greek architecture; and, appearing to be suffering from mild indigestion, Miss Garvie fluttered her fingers to her mouth. Kit smothered a yawn then, catching Georgie's eye, felt a slow burning under his ribs which had nothing to do with indigestion and everything to do with being unable to jump to his feet and carry her off to somewhere more private.

As though reading his thoughts, Georgie hurriedly looked away.

Kit tried to turn his attention back to Mrs Ashton, who by this stage was talking about Lord Byron. As if he knew anything about Lord Byron! He nodded politely and once more let his eyes stray along the other occupants of the table until his gaze rested on his father's. A feeling of such complete understanding flowed between them that Kit was momentarily dumbfounded. He gave a slow, wide grin. Papa looked from his face to Georgie's and smiled back.

At last dinner was over and the ladies left the room. The port appeared, but Papa's glass remained untouched. 'I hope you will forgive me,' he said, 'if I leave you gentlemen to it. Feeling a trifle under the weather. No, please don't get up. My son Kit will see me through to the library. I'll join you later when I'm feeling more the thing.'

Kit was immediately on his feet. 'Papa?' His voice was all concern.

'Now, don't fuss me. Nothing wrong.'

'Glad to hear it, Papa,' said Kit in a tone which belied his words. Briskly — but, due to his weakened shoulder, with some difficulty — he manoeuvred the chair from the dining room and towards the library.

Papa gave a chuckle. 'Found the conversation boring. Rather be alone with my son, and what's wrong with that?'

'Nothing . . . But kindly do me the service of not worrying me in that way again!'

Once they were in the library and Grey, the old lurcher, had begrudgingly offered up his space in front of the fire and next to his master, Kit poured two tots of brandy and passed one to his father.

'Like your Miss Rankin,' Papa said

suddenly into the silence. 'Tell her she can sketch me some more if she has the inclination. Like her better than that wittering Garvie woman. She drives me demented with her dithering ways.'

'Quite!'

'She's a Langley, you know.'

'Who? Miss Garvie?'

'No, young Miss Rankin . . . She won't have anything to do with them, though; of course she won't. Treated her mother shabbily because she chose a love-match over family dictates. Don't suppose they've heard of George Rankin's death.' He stared at the fire morosely. 'Don't suppose they'd have done anything even if they had. Shame. She's a spirited girl, Miss Rankin. Like her. Like her very much.'

'Yes, so do I,' said Kit.

He was treated to a bristling look. 'Thought you did. Hardly know her yet, though. Still, sometimes that's how it is. Quick. Like a thunderbolt.'

'Quite!' said a slightly bewildered Kit again.

'It was like that for George Rankin. I knew the Langley girl — vaguely . . . Lovely girl, society adored her. All set to make a good marriage. Then along came this ramshackle painter fellow . . . Next thing we heard, they'd run off together to London! Harrumph! When Ashton recommended him to paint you, all those years later, I kept quiet about any involvement I'd had with his wife's family. Met up with George in London and — well, I liked him, we had a chat, I discovered his wife had died, and he said he had a son who worked as his young apprentice; never mentioned a daughter at the time . . . Hmm; funny, that.'

Kit opened his mouth, then closed it again. Georgie's secret wasn't his to tell.

'Rankin had a certain spirit and a lot of charm. Took to him, so I engaged him to paint you. Made a good job of it too. You know the rest.' He gave Kit a sharp glance. 'Wouldn't want you to upset Miss Rankin,' he said. 'Wouldn't want you to bring her

214

name into disrepute.'

It was Kit's turn to bristle; although, he acknowledged, he didn't do quite such a good job of it as his father — maybe his eyebrows weren't yet mature. Nevertheless, he tried his best. 'I assure you, sir, nothing could be further from my mind. I hold that lady in great esteem. I admire the way she has risen above her circumstances, and I've, well . . . ' Damn it. What was he thinking? He'd nearly told Papa he was in love with her!

A searching look was directed at him from under the bushy eyebrows. 'Hmm. Thought that was the way of it, so just as well to make my thoughts clear on the subject. Don't want to see any hanky-panky going on. Not the thing, Kit, not the thing at all. The girl's got good lineage! Might make a good marriage, wouldn't do to spoil her chances.'

Kit smiled. 'I have no dishonourable intentions towards the lady. You may have my word on it.'

'There's another thing,' said Papa, after a pause in which he scratched the lurcher's grizzled head. 'That cousin of Arabella's. Something about him I don't like. Prefer to send him packing ... Can't do that, though; Arabella seems amused by him, and he's kept the estate ticking over ... Still, now you're back. Different circumstances ... Harrumph! Damned if I see why I should put up with him any longer. Not in this house, anyway. Thought it would be a good thing — get him out from under my feet — give him a property on the estate. Fair enough, eh? But he doesn't seem keen.'

'Well ... '

'I know. I'd rather he went altogether. Don't like the fellow. Never have. Making eyes at Arabella at every opportunity. Damned impudence ... Of course, she'll have none of him. Knows where to draw the line. Likes her flirts, but that's as far as it goes ... Devoted to me and the children! Devoted!'

'Indeed,' agreed Kit, mentally crossing his fingers.

'Damned if I won't do it,' went on
Papa. 'Not immediately. But once
you're settled in, got the bit between
your teeth, I'll get rid of him.'

'Papa, is that quite fair?'

Papa's eyebrows rose and his voice
with them. 'Quite fair? You're asking me
if it's *quite fair*?'

'Hugo's done a tremendous amount
for the estate, Papa. I expected the
place to be quite run down.'

'Run down?' Papa's eyebrows
bristled again and his voice went up
another octave. The lurcher lifted his
head in disquiet. 'Why would you
think that? I paid him, didn't I? And I
paid him well . . . *Am* paying him well!
He gets his keep and a very nice way
of life. Three years he's been here. I'll
grant you he's done a good job, but so
he should have with what I pay him
. . . Far and above a normal estate
manager's wages, let me tell you! Far
and above.'

'Right,' said Kit. 'It just seems a little unfair.'

'UNFAIR?' Papa's voice was thunderous now and his face had gone an alarming colour. 'I'm still the master in this house; *I'll* say what's fair and what's unfair.'

Holding his hands up in defeat, Kit leaned back in his chair and tried for a relaxed smile. 'Papa, there's no need to be in such a taking. We've time to decide on these things. There's nothing to rush for . . . Now, we have guests, and we don't want them to think we have fallen out already, when nothing could be further from the truth.'

The lurcher turned his head just enough to look reproachfully at Kit, then settled down again in prime position on the hearthrug.

'Harrumph! Well. Maybe I'm over-hasty, but I don't mind telling you, Kit — that fellow makes my flesh crawl the way he creeps round the place, smirking all the while. But you're right. I have only to bear it a little longer, and tonight we have guests and we must join them shortly and make good conversation.'

A relieved sigh escaped Kit's lips as, after a discreet knock, Brewer entered and asked if he could assist Mr Merryfield to the drawing room.

He was holding the door to the library open to allow Brewer to push the chair through when a slight movement further down the passage caught his eye. There was something furtive about the movement, as though the person would rather not be noticed.

Kit scowled. He couldn't be certain, but something was telling him it had been Hugo lurking in the shadows to see what he might learn.

8

By the time Georgiana finally reached her bedchamber that evening, she felt so exhausted she could hardly manage to remove her clothes. Although her olive gown fitted snugly with a front fastening that was designed to enable her to dress without assistance, hooks refused to become unhooked and bone buttons, small as they were, impossible to release. It suddenly seemed, together with the day's events, just too much.

Physically drained, nerves stretched to breaking point, she gave up on the buttons, sat down on her bed, and tried to make some sort of sense of it all.

First, there'd been the morning encounter with Kit, where she'd allowed him to come too close and act in far too familiar a fashion; putting his hand over hers, gazing into her eyes and the like. She knew she was weak, knew it was wrong

. . . so why had she subsequently permitted him to talk her into asking to draw Joshua Merryfield? That could surely be only an added complication.

Second, during the painting session with the children, she'd let herself be enticed into a confrontation with Lizzie when, as a teacher, she should have been above such things. Then there had been the rebuffing of Hugo's advances, feeble though they were. That had been annoying and unnecessary.

As if that weren't enough, in keeping her promise to Kit, after luncheon she'd bearded Joshua Merryfield in his den, and was just congratulating herself on making a half-decent likeness of him when he'd sprung on her the news that he had known her mother and her mother's family! As if she would want to know anything about that. As if she would want to ever go to them with cap in hand. No, she most certainly wouldn't! What she *would* like to do, if ever she became rich and famous, would be to turn down a commission to paint a Langley portrait. Wouldn't that be satisfying? 'I do apologise, Lady Hermione, but my mother would not have approved. The Langleys refused to acknowledge her, you see, once she'd married a *mere* artist . . . No, it's of no use to plead or cry, my sensibilities just would not allow it.'

Oh, how pleasant that would be!

But that was a dream. In reality, later in that same, seemingly *week*, of a day, there had been Kit and that kiss! Then there was the escape to her room, only to be interrupted by Jane insisting that she came to meet the guests. As a result of which, perhaps the most frightening thing of all occurred. A direct encounter with Squire Ashton, who clearly had grave doubts about being told that he'd never met her before! And well might he have doubts! 'I never forget a face,' he'd said. Georgie shivered. Somehow she'd known he was not a man who would give up easily.

Barely had she got over that trauma when Kit had chosen the very next moment to mouth *I love you* to her!

Momentarily she shut her eyes as though in pain. Why did he have to do that? What did he expect her to do about it? She supposed he must think it was highly diverting to see just how easy it would be to make some little nobody of an art teacher fall head over heels in love with him. That must be it — it couldn't possibly be true.

Her face burned. There was no denying it would be a good way of paying her back for daring to create a nude image of him four years ago!

Ruthlessly, she dismissed the memory of them standing facing one another; she in boy's knee breeches, her cap on the floor, her hair a fiery cloud around her head; he in a too-big uniform, staring at her in shocked disgust.

Her face burned some more.

After that, there had been tea in the schoolroom with Miss Garvie and Josh to be endured. And subsequently the prospect of, as the evening's endurance test, another of those interminable dinners with the family and guests.

Georgiana had taken some deep breaths, changed into her olive-green dress, and allowed Betsy to dress her hair. Then she'd tapped on Miss Garvie's door and, avoiding Squire Ashton's bright inquiring eyes, made polite conversation in the drawing room before sitting straight-backed and tense through dinner.

Admittedly, once she'd returned to the drawing room with the other ladies, she'd felt a momentary sense of relief. Over half the evening was completed. Perhaps she was safe.

But had she been safe?

She'd not counted on Squire Ashton.

Engaged in a trivial conversation with the doctor's wife regarding childhood illnesses, Georgie was just relaxing a little when from the corner of her eye she saw Squire Ashton and Kit approach the group. The odd idea that Kit fancied himself as her protector presented itself.

'Miss Rankin, did you say your

brother was younger or older than you?'
asked Squire Ashton when there was a
break in the conversation.

Oh Lord! As if matters could get any
worse, on a waft of perfume, Arabella
drifted over.

Georgie thought quickly and opened
her mouth to say 'younger'.

'Oh, older,' said Kit.

Georgie shut her mouth again. *Drat
Kit; he thought he was helping.*

'Strange *he* wasn't called George,
then? I'm sure I remember Rankin
saying he his son was named George,
after him, and he called him Georgie to
avoid confusion. You know — eldest son
named after his father, that's the usual
way of things?' The squire leaned back
on his heels with a satisfied expression.

'Not at all,' said Kit. 'Not called
Joshua, am I? That's my younger
brother's name, as you well know . . .
Bit of an old-fashioned thing to do,
isn't it? Not to mention, as you say,
confusing to boot.'

Georgie wondered where on earth all

this was leading. He was overstating the case; making it worse by the second.

'Papa's known as Joshua, my brother's just Josh. What's wrong with that?' went on Kit, sounding a little desperate. 'I expect they never thought of it first time round. You know — calling me Josh, not Joshua . . . ' He looked round at the puzzled faces. 'Shouldn't ask Papa about it, though. He'd not be amused. It seemed my mother wanted me called Christopher.'

Arabella seemed about to speak, shot a glance at Georgie, and changed her mind.

And was it Georgie's imagination, or was Mrs Bainbridge looking at Kit as though he were speaking a foreign language?

It was no good, she'd have to say something. 'As I told you before, my brother's name was Thomas, not George,' she stated in a cool voice. 'They didn't think he would live . . . He did, of course, but not for as long as I should have liked . . . because now, you see, I have no one.' She very nearly followed this up with a pathetic sniff but, from somewhere behind her, Doctor Bainbridge cleared his throat.

'Weather seems set to get worse, snowflakes are bigger and the drifts are piling up.'

Dear Doctor Bainbridge, Georgie resolved to remember him in her prayers.

'Oh, I do hope not,' said Arabella with a small laugh. 'Although the children will love it, of course . . . But should the bottom road become blocked, you and Mrs Bainbridge are very welcome to stay until it's cleared, Doctor; and the reverend too, of course.'

So the moment had passed. Card tables had been set up for the older members of the party. Jane, Prudence and Charles had gathered around the pianoforte at the far end of the drawing room, and Georgie allowed herself to be coerced into singing a duet with Jane. It was a song they'd sung together many times before at the academy, so although her rendition was a little shaky, she had no trouble in remembering the words.

The evening wore on — and on.

Avoiding contact with any male member of the party as much as possible, Georgiana kept in the background for the remainder of the torturous evening. When yet more refreshments arrived, she made herself useful in handing them round, and was rewarded with a searching look from Mr Merryfield and a nod from his wife. After this, and as soon as she could reasonably do so, she made her way back to Arabella's side, expressed her thanks for a pleasant evening and, more or less, asked if she might retire.

Permission was given with a charming smile. 'You have a very pretty voice, Miss Rankin. Sleep well.'

'Thank you,' replied Miss Rankin, well-behaved young schoolteacher who knew her place. Gratefully and speedily, she made her escape.

With a wry smile and a sigh, Georgie

brought herself back to the present. She once more tackled the unyielding bone buttons. At long last the evening was over; she could don her nightgown, shake out her hair, and forget it!

But how bird-witted of her to have ever thought it would be easy!

In her innocence, she'd thought to escort Jane home to Yorkshire and spend a sennight or two painting a cosy family portrait in luxurious surroundings. Being fed well, enjoying the experience as a little holiday, perhaps; and, at the end, being paid handsomely. She smiled again at how naïve in retrospect that thought seemed. Even if Kit had not been here, she would still have had Squire Ashton to contend with!

Finally the olive-green gown submitted to its unfastenings. Shaking out any creases, she draped it over a chair and pulled back the covers on her inviting-looking bed.

In spite of everything, she had survived. The sheets felt fresh and smelled faintly of lavender. With a faint curve to her lips, and the vision of Kit's face refusing to disappear from her brain, she drifted into an exhausted sleep.

Only a few hours later, she struggled awake. There was some sort of disturbance going on. Doors were opening and closing; there was a muffled cry; then the sound of hurried footsteps in the outside passage.

She lifted her head from her pillow. What was going on?

Well, whatever it was, it had nothing to do with her. Did it?

It was warm and cosy in her bed. She'd earned her rest. There was no need for her to interfere in any way. No need at all.

Absolutely none!

'Drat and double drat!' She lit her bedside candle, rose from her bed and, draping her shawl around her shoulders, opened her door a crack. From where she was she could see that Jane's door was also ajar. Georgie crept over to it and pushed it further. Jane's bed was empty.

A gasp of breath sounded behind her. Miss Garvie, encased in a nightgown which started at her chin, ended an inch above the floor, and was further covered by a woollen pelisse, stood there with the light of her candle showing a panic-stricken face below a lace nightcap pulled down to her eyebrows.

'What's happening?' asked Georgie.

'I — I don't know. I was awoken by some strange cries but I didn't dare get out of my bed until I heard you . . . Where's Jane? She's not in her room.' Her voice tailed off on a whimper, then her eyes looked beyond Georgie. 'Oh l-look, there's a glow at the end of the corridor. D-d'you think there's a f-fire?'

Amidst more sounds of frenzied activity coming from the main area of the house, Georgie sniffed the air. 'I think that's just the light from a flickering candle. I can't smell smoke

. . . Are the other children awake?'

Miss Garvie looked round furtively. 'I don't think so. Lizzie and Prudence and Josh are further down this end of the corridor, and Charles is in the other wing.'

'No point in waking them,' said Georgie. 'Look, you stay here in case we need to wake them and get them out down the back stairs. I'll go and see what I can find out.'

'Oh dear, d'you think you should? What if . . . ' Miss Garvie's twittering voice trailed off.

'What if *what*?' said Georgie, a trifle impatiently. 'I'm only going to see what all the fuss is about. If it's nothing to do with us, I'll just come back again, no harm done, and we can all sleep easy in our beds.'

'Oh, Miss Rankin, I wish I could be more like you. You always know what to do.'

Georgie very nearly snorted. 'I'll take your candle, if I may. It has more wax left, mine's nearly burned through; but please take it. Chances are it's nothing much, and I'll be back in a trice.'

'Yes, yes, of course. Have my candle, I have another spare in my room. I'll wait here for you until you come back.'

With a heart beating slightly faster than usual, Georgie set off towards the source of the commotion. At the end of the passage she reached a landing table where a candelabra was burning and the door to a further corridor had been left open. Coming from the darkness beyond, she heard another groan. It sounded like a man's voice. Tentatively, she walked a few more steps. Even further along there was some activity was taking place. Wavering candlelight; a group of people, shadows and whispers.

Another feeble, groaning sigh made her stop in her tracks, goosebumps suddenly forming on her arms. Whatever this was, it clearly had nothing to do with her. Other people were involved, everything must be under control. As long as the children were safe, that was the extent of her and Miss Garvie's responsibilities.

About to make her way back to her bedchamber, she turned. As she did so, a shape detached itself from the shadowy group ahead and came towards her. Shading the candle, she shrunk back into the gloom.

The shape metamorphosed into Kit. He was wearing a frog-fastened dressing jacket and a distraught expression.

He gave a start. 'Georgie! You gave me a fright . . . I thought I heard a sound and it might be one of the children.'

'Sorry, Kit.' She swallowed. 'I heard something and it sounded, I don't know — not something to be ignored. I came to see what the matter is and whether there's anything I can do.'

'Thank you, Georgie, but no. Papa has had a bad turn. Much worse than usual, apparently. His man called on Doctor Bainbridge who's with him now. Arabella is quite distressed, but I must say not as hysterical as I feared.

Jane is also here now, which helps.'

'Yes' said Georgie. 'That was why I came, really. She left her door open and I could see her bed was empty, and, well . . . '

Kit's worried frown lightened a little. 'Well, there is nothing to do about it and he is in good hands. Bainbridge seems to think it was too much rich food, but I've never seen Papa in such pain or so sick. Thank God Bainbridge was here.'

He peered at her more closely. Instinctively, Georgie tightened her shawl round her shoulders.

'You're shaking,' he said, putting his good arm around her. 'Come, I'll take you back to your room, then I'll come back for Jane.'

His hand rested on her shoulder, the touch of it burning through the shawl and her cambric nightgown to her skin. For a moment, she wanted his hand to stay there for ever. 'No, no,' she said. 'I can go back alone. Now I know what's amiss and that we are not all about to be burnt in our beds as Miss Garvie feared . . . '

'Burned in our beds?'

'Just a strange fancy she had. No, go back to your Pa and your family. They need you. If there's anything I can do, of course . . . '

For a long moment their eyes held. 'There's so much, so much . . . ' He shook his head as though to clear his thoughts. 'But not now. Not tonight.'

He lifted a curl and stroked it through his fingers. 'Your hair is as beautiful as ever,' he said and, leaning forward, dropped a feather-light kiss on her brow. 'Now, go back to bed and I will see you in the morning. I think I'll be sitting up with Papa tonight.'

Feeling as though this must have been the very longest and most eventful day of her life, Georgiana turned and set off back down the corridor to reassure Miss Garvie. After a little more twittering, Miss Garvie, whose teeth were chattering either with fright or with cold, did not take much persuading to go back to her room

Georgie lay awake until, a few moments later, she heard Kit return with Jane; then, admonishing herself not to read too much into that very sweet but disturbing brush of Kit's lips on her forehead, she once more closed her eyes . . .

★　★　★

Kit walked back to where Arabella, Jane and Doctor Bainbridge stood speaking together in hushed tones just outside the door of Papa's bed chamber.

'Ah Kit,' said Arabella immediately she saw him. 'I am so glad you're here. Papa is sleeping lightly now, but is still very weak.' Distractedly, she put her hand to her brow. 'I can't understand how he can so suddenly have become so ill. The doctor thinks food poisoning, but we all ate the same. No one else has showed signs of illness . . . Unless — '
Her voice suddenly sharpened with

anxiety. 'Who was that you spoke to? Are the children all right?'

'The children are sleeping soundly — apart from Jane, of course. No, it was Miss Rankin we heard. She and Miss Garvie woke and realised something was amiss, and wondered if they could help in any way.'

Arabella nodded.

'Miss Rankin is good in a crisis,' said Jane. 'She always knows what's best to be done.'

Kit cast a glance in Arabella's direction. 'You look greatly fatigued, ma'am. Now Papa's sleeping I think you should get some rest. I'll take Jane back now, then come and sit with him.'

'I can sit with him,' said Arabella with a wave of her hand. 'There's not much I can do for him these days except amuse him now and then. The least I can do is sit with him when he has need of me. Besides, I should like to be here when he wakes.'

'We'll sit together then,' said Kit after giving her a long appraising glance.

'Then the doctor can rest and one of us can fetch him should he be needed.'

Again Arabella nodded. Her face looked shocked and pale but she seemed steady and in control.

'Right,' said Kit turning to his sister. 'Come along, young lady, you need to catch up with your sleep.'

'Kit, Papa will be alright won't he?' asked Jane quietly as they walked back to the nursery wing.

'Oh, assuredly so,' answered Kit.

'Only Doctor Bainbridge did seem quite puzzled as well as worried. He said the sickness was very severe.'

'But he's sleeping peacefully enough now. He's probably exhausted, what with my return, the party tonight, and the rich food.' Jane still looked very unsure. Kit gave her a brotherly squeeze. 'Oh, I know he's infirm on the outside, but he's strong inside. It's just a spell of sickness; he'll come about, you'll see.'

But despite his reassurances to Jane, it was with a set face that he rejoined

Arabella in his father's bedchamber.

After instructing them to call him if there was the slightest change, Doctor Bainbridge had gone back to rest and Kit and his stepmother were left sitting one each side of the bed.

Arabella was holding his father's hand. 'I don't understand it,' she muttered. 'I don't understand it at all. He enjoyed this evening. He told me so. He was laughing, and enjoyed a debate with the reverend and with Squire Ashton, and of course he's taken a liking to Miss Rankin — as have we all.'

Kit refrained from comment.

'He enjoyed his dinner — and his glass of brandy. Didn't complain of indigestion, but I'm told he took his medicine as a preventive measure. But this sickness — it's just so unlike him ... Oh, his back aches and he gets short of breath, he gets impatient with himself and sometimes wakes up with cramps, but not sickness, and not like that ... ' She shuddered and looked again at her husband's pale face. 'He will be alright, Kit, won't he?'

'Oh, assuredly so,' said Kit, feeling rather like a parrot. 'You know what he's like. Looks frail but has the constitution of an ox. Take more than a bout of sickness to incapacitate him for long.'

Arabella gave him a wan smile. 'I meant it earlier when I said I was glad you're here. I am, Kit, *very* glad.'

'Well, so am I.'

For a few moments it was quiet save for the steady sound of his father's breathing.

'I suppose you don't think much of me,' said Arabella. 'I suppose I'm not a very worthy character — always thinking of myself, always wanting fresh amusements . . . Marriage isn't as I expected. Oh, I knew your father was older than me, I knew he'd worshipped your mother, I knew it would be an uphill struggle to make you accept me — and that was all I wanted, really, your acceptance. And then the children came along — you seemed to like them, at least. But I wished you could have liked me.'

Kit shrugged. 'I expect I should have tried harder.'

There was another silence. Did she expect him to wipe out the bitterness of being usurped in his father's affections and being disregarded in his own home? Did she expect him to conveniently forget all the times when he was a raw eighteen-year-old that she'd brushed up against him a little too closely, or cast him beguiling looks from under her lashes?

'Then, with the accident . . . ' Arabella went on. ' . . . well, it was difficult. I've always been easily bored, and your father — well, he wanted a different life then. Hated seeing his old friends in London, always talking about the things he could no longer do. We both tried hard to come to terms with things as they were. I'd come to the marriage thinking he would indulge me, look after me . . . And, well, none of that was any longer possible. It seemed best I sometimes went to London alone and at least picked up some semblance of my old life there. It — it didn't mean I loved your father any the less. In fact, when I came back, things would be easier for a while.'

'I'm sure.'

'Oh, why should I expect you to understand? You're young, you have no idea.'

Kit struggled for something to say. 'Thank you for not saying that I was named for Papa, and that his first name is actually Christopher,' he said eventually.

'Hmm, Squire Ashton thinks he knows everything. I enjoyed seeing you take the wind out of his sails.'

There was only the sound of Papa's ragged breathing, and after a while Kit realised that Arabella had dosed off. He stared at her, observing, now her face was in repose, how a few fine lines had crept around her eyes and that her jawline had become softer. In sleep, her face lost its vivacity and sparkle

— became that of a weary thirty-five-year-old woman.

'Kit, is that you?' The feeble voice came out of the dimness. Immediately, Kit leaned across. His father's bright eyes were staring at him from the hollows surrounding them.

'Papa. No, don't try to talk, but are you feeling more the thing?' He cursed himself and gave a twisted smile. 'No, don't answer that. Let me get you a drink.'

In spite of the fact that his lips looked cracked and parched, Mr Merryfield lifted a weak hand in refusal. 'Felt better, lad,' he said. 'But not so curst nauseous as I did.'

'You frightened us all ... Is there anything you need? Shall I call Bainbridge?'

'No need. Not yet, anyway. Not going to pop my clogs just yet, although ... ' His voice petered out.

Kit gave a grin. 'That's the spirit.'

Mr Merryfield closed his eyes but gave a wan smile. 'Was going to say might be the best way. You'll manage the place. I have complete trust in you.'

'Joshua!' It was Arabella.

His eyelids opened. 'You still here, my love? I've given you a right fright tonight . . . Kept you from your bed.'

Arabella bent over him and solicitously adjusted the bedcovers. 'As if I care for a few winks of sleep . . . But don't talk. Shall I fetch Doctor Bainbridge?' she asked, unconsciously repeating Kit's mistake.

'No, but perhaps a little water now . . . '

Something made Kit allow Arabella to be the one to lift the glass to his father's lips. 'Just a sip, my love,' she said.

The effort of lifting his head to sip at the glass seemed to drain Papa of his remaining strength, and he collapsed back against the pillows with a sigh. 'Go to bed, my sweet,' he whispered. 'You have guests in the morning. I am on the mend, I promise you. I just need rest now.'

Arabella leaned over and gently kissed his brow.

By the time she stood up, Papa was asleep again.

Kit and his stepmother stood on either side of the bed, staring at one another. 'You should do as he says,' said Kit eventually. 'I'll stay here and watch him. I'm very used to disturbed nights.'

'You must call me immediately should you need me. *Immediately*, you understand!'

'I will,' promised Kit, and watched as Arabella, obviously still anxious but determined to hide the fact, quietly left the room.

He sank into a half-sleep and came to to find that Doctor Bainbridge was in the room bending over the invalid. Dimly, he was aware of the early-morning sounds of the house coming to life. He stretched, inadvertently yawning as he did so.

Doctor Bainbridge glanced over his shoulder. 'He had a good night, then? There appears to be no fever, thank

God. Your father has a robust constitution despite everything.'

'So it seems,' agreed Kit. 'Unusual for him to cast up his accounts. Never remember it happening before.' His eye rested on the medicine bottle on the side table. 'But obviously he's been having some digestive problems of late?'

The doctor frowned. 'Nothing like this. I don't like it . . . ' He shot Kit a probing glance. 'I'd like a quiet word outside. Don't want to disturb him now he's sleeping peacefully.'

At once Kit was all attention.

'You were saying?' They were standing outside his father's door and talking in subdued tones.

Doctor Bainbridge shifted his stance. 'Of late, I have been worried about your Papa's state of mind. He's often appeared morose and entirely dispirited.'

'Yes, you said as much this evening when we met. I must say, I hadn't noticed it. Since I returned, at least, he has appeared quite his old self despite his apparent fragility.'

'On yesterday's performance, yes, I would agree with you — but over the past few months, I must confess to seeing him more blue-devilled than ever before. It was almost as though he'd given up on life.'

Kit frowned. Papa? Give up on life? Never!

'But then,' continued the doctor, 'when I saw him last evening, smiling and conversing with us all, looking at you with such pride, paying attention to Miss Rankin — to whom he seems to have taken a shine — I thought he was perhaps at the end of the darkness that had set upon him. But now — this! I must confess when I was called to the scene by your stepmama and I saw the severity of his sickness, my first thought was that it had been self-induced. That he had somehow got hold of a noxious substance and tried to end his life.'

'No!' At once Kit's every instinct rushed to the fore. 'Trust me on this. He wouldn't do that . . . He would never do that to his family ... He would not,' he repeated firmly. 'I know he would not.'

Doctor Bainbridge regarded him through world-weary eyes. 'I have known a great many who have, Kit — many who have. But no, not this time. The timing is all wrong. He had turned the corner. You're right. His eldest son had just returned home, something he had been praying for. He would want to get to know you again. Anyway, how would he have had access to enough poison to bring about that effect? I must be wrong, and yet ... '

'Poison? What do you mean — poison?'

'Something nasty. My first thought was arsenic. Bound to be some about. The gardeners would need it for weedkiller and keeping the rats out of the compost. House this size, with its cellars and store cupboards? Feasible, surely?'

Still unable to believe such a thing, Kit turned away. 'But how would he?'

He turned back accusingly. 'You said it yourself. He's in a chair with wheels which is the very devil to operate. He has to be carried up and down stairs, which is why his bedchamber is so conveniently placed near the library, study, drawing and dining rooms . . . How could he have managed to obtain it? No, the whole thing is totally untenable.'

'No need to get into a lather about it, Kit — you must see I had to share my fears with someone.'

'Yes, well; you're wrong, that's all. You're wrong. It must have been something he ate.'

'No-one else has been ill, and the reaction was so very severe I find it difficult to believe it was the food, unless something was put on your father's plate alone. I watched him being served from the same dishes as myself . . . I don't mind telling you, Kit, I'm not happy about the situation. Not happy at all.'

'What's amiss now?' It was a

pinch-faced Arabella, clad in a silk robe and a hurriedly-thrown-on woollen shawl. 'Tell me he is still sleeping, tell me he is much recovered.'

'You may rest easy; your husband is much better and in no pain. You may sit with him, but please don't disturb him with questions; his strength is at a low ebb.'

Arabella's shoulders sank with relief. Then her eyes narrowed. 'So why are you whispering, and why were you saying you were not happy? I don't understand.'

Thinking speedily even as he spoke, Kit gave a smile that he hoped was reassuring. 'Lord, ma'am, we're all tired. Doctor Bainbridge was talking about the weather, deeming it necessary for him to stay longer and have no access to his surgery and the books that would assist him in diagnosing Papa's sickness. Isn't that right, Bainbridge?'

He looked questioningly at Doctor Bainbridge, who obligingly nodded.

Arabella rolled her eyes. 'What does

that matter? The main thing is that Joshua is on the mend. I'll just sit with him a little to be sure he is truly well. Then I suppose I must dress and attend my guests.'

As she closed the door behind her, the doctor's hand landed on Kit's good shoulder. 'You should try and get some rest too. I'll take charge now, and get his man to sit with him . . . '

Noticing the doctor's worried expression, Kit felt a moment's contrition. 'Thank you for all you've done, Doctor. If I was short earlier, I apologise. I don't want you to feel I'm ungrateful . . . '

'It's still a puzzle, Kit, and I don't like puzzles.'

Kit didn't like puzzles either, especially not when they involved the health of his father. 'I'll think on it!'

It wasn't until — after instructing Jenkins to wake him no later than ten o'clock — he wearily lay himself down on his bed that it occurred to him that if the doctor was so sure poison was involved in his father's sudden sickness, then it could equally well be someone other than Papa who had administered the dose . . .

9

You would never guess, thought Georgiana, that Arabella had been up half the night worrying about her husband. Watching her now, presiding over breakfast, as vivacious as always and every bit as though she had a full eight hours' sleep behind her, she felt a stirring of respect for her hostess.

Mr Merryfield was never at breakfast, and there was no comment over the fact that neither Kit nor the doctor was present. Breakfast in big houses, she had learned, was something to be taken as and when, with individuals helping themselves from the dishes set out on the side board. Markington Hall was no exception, and Georgie took her cue from Miss Garvie, appearing in the breakfast room, along with the children, some time after eight but certainly before nine in the morning. Guests and family members might do otherwise, but it was an unwritten rule for those in the Merryfields' service to be finished by nine-thirty.

This morning, there had been a swift whispered conversation between Miss Garvie, Jane and Georgiana. 'Mama sent her maid to tell me Papa, though weak, is recovering, and we are not to mention last night's troubles to our guests,' Jane had said quickly before Lizzie or Josh joined them.

Georgie and Miss Garvie nodded to each other in relief, then both concentrated on keeping the children's natural high spirits at the sight of so much snow and the thought of tobogganing at a level befitting a house which has recently seen sickness.

When they arrived at breakfast it was to find that the Ashton family was not yet present. With a feeling of disappointment Georgiana noticed that neither was Kit.

But then, what would she say to him

anyway? *Good morning, Kit. By the way, did you mean it when you said you loved me, or were you just amusing yourself?*

However, the Reverend Richards was before them, and was voicing his concerns over those of his parishioners to whom he had promised morning visits. Mrs Bainbridge was more down-to-earth.

'They have only to look out of the window to see it is out of the question,' she said. 'It's the same with the doctor's patients. As I told him this morning, they will just have to wait. It won't be the first time we've been snowed in, goodness knows.'

'Indeed,' said Arabella, 'Although word is that there'll be no more today. The men are to attempt clearing a way through to the bottom road, so hopefully by tomorrow at least you should be able to reach your homes ... Not that you are not, as always, very welcome to stay for as long as ever you would like ... '

Considering that Arabella very probably wished all her guests at Jericho, Georgiana developed an even stronger admiration for her ability to put manners and hospitality above all else.

At this moment, a pale-faced Hugo entered the room.

'Good heavens, Hugo, you look rather out of sorts,' said the reverend.

'To tell the truth, I do feel a little knocked up,' said Hugo, licking his for once unsmiling lips and sliding into his place.

'Looks as sick as a cushion,' said Josh, earning a frown from Jane and an intake of breath from Miss Garvie — who was, thought Georgie, born to be shocked.

'Well, I only said . . . Anyway, where's Kit? He said he'd come and see the puppies. Particularly Bouncer. He's a plucky little fellow — he'll be a great ratter.'

'Kit is wounded, Josh, as you well know,' Jane said quickly. 'You have to be patient. I'd have thought with all the snow out there you'd be thinking on rescuing the old sled and taking it to the dipping, and I'm sure if you build a snowman above the ha-ha, Papa would like no end to see it from his window.'

'Mama, do we have to have our portraits painted today?' asked Lizzie in a voice so plaintive it made Georgie want to smack her.

'That depends on Miss Rankin.'

'I was planning to work today, but I can do so from my sketchbook. It would be useful, though, to have access to the gowns you would like your daughters to wear. Something pastel might be fitting?'

'I see,' replied Arabella, in tones that implied she didn't take too kindly to receiving recommendations from the hired help. 'And what do you propose *I* wear?'

Oh dear, a disturbed night's rest hadn't done anything to reduce Arabella's acidity if she felt anyone to be rising above their station. Georgiana thought quickly. 'The ideal,' she suggested, 'would be a gown of a slightly darker hue than the girls' dresses. Maybe a deeper rose — if you have a gown of that description ... Um, Jane has already told me she'd like to wear her cream-coloured muslin; and Lizzie, we thought, in a pale pink. At their feet, Josh would be in a light shirt and waistcoat, with perhaps dark knee-breeches?'

For a long moment Arabella stared across at her. 'Indeed. You are very exacting in your requirements, Miss Rankin. One might almost think you on a par with George Romney, whom I believe was quite dictatorial about the dress of his subjects in order to achieve his desired effect.'

She lifted a daintily-sized morsel of ham to her lips and chewed it slowly. 'What kind of effect are you hoping to achieve?'

Georgie felt her face heat up. What was it Pa had said on examining a small study of a mother and son that she had executed? 'You could become an excellent forger, Georgie. Your style is romantic, yet simple.' His eyes had twinkled. 'What's more, your initials are the very same. G.R. in the corner! Well to remember that, if ever you hit hard times. He's dead too, always an advantage; died at Kendal beginning of the century.' He slapped his knee and chuckled. 'Take it to an obscure art dealer, introduce yourself under a false name, pretend you were left it by an aunt — no idea where it came from! The initials? Well, maybe you'd heard of a George — what was it, Reynolds? No, he was a Joshua — Romney? By Jupiter! Any dealer who knows anything would snap your fingers off.'

An upward lift twitched at her lips as she recalled the outrageous conversation. But Arabella was waiting for an answer — now!

'It might sound a little sentimental, Mrs Merryfield, but the effect I'm after is of your family forming a rose with you at the centre: the girls as the outer, paler petals . . . '

'I'm not like a rose,' said Joshua hotly. 'I won't be a sissy rose petal!'

'Of course not. You're the thorny stem,' said Lizzie with a snigger.

Arabella looked fondly at her son. 'No, but the foliage, perhaps? A male foil to our femininity.' She gave an indulgent smile. 'You don't have to be so literal, my love . . . Hmm, I rather like the concept of myself as the centre of a rose. How very clever of you, Miss Rankin.'

Miss Rankin thought so too, and breathed a sigh of relief.

'And what about Bouncer, where will he be?'

'Bouncer?'

'My new puppy, Mama. He can be in it too. Miss Rankin said she was used to drawing the overindulged pets, and she'd be glad to paint Bouncer in the stables and put him in the picture afterwards.'

Arabella's eyebrows rose. 'Did she indeed?' Then she gave a tired smile. 'Oh, why not? I'm sure you know what will work, Miss Rankin, you seem quite competent.'

Georgie knew how to accept a compliment, however begrudging, and kept her eyes downcast. 'Thank you.'

'Now, I have things to do,' said Arabella. She looked across at Hugo. 'Perhaps you should discuss the nature of your indisposition with the doctor, Hugo; you do appear rather out of sorts . . . ' She turned away, but not before Georgie had read in her expression the fleeting idea that there might be some connection between her husband's violent sickness and Hugo's sudden malady. Arabella, however, continued as though no such thought had occurred. 'I trust you children and Miss Garvie to organize your morning — we could do with some peace and quiet today!'

After Arabella had left the room, Lizzie glanced across at Jane. 'I've never heard Mama wish for peace and quiet in all of my life.'

'There's always a first time,' said

Jane. 'Maybe she has the headache.'

Lizzie gave a snort, and suddenly Georgie found herself liking her better. 'I've never known her to have a headache when we have guests! Something's happened to upset her.'

'No, well . . . ' Jane paused as Charles came in. 'Oh, good morning Charles.' With interest, Georgie watched Jane's pretty blush as Charles gave her a grin and took a seat beside her.

Lizzie noticed too, and gave her brother a knowing look.

It was clearly lost on him.

'The sledge,' said Josh. 'I think Charles and I should see if we can find it.'

*   *   *

Having satisfied himself that Papa, though shockingly debilitated, was otherwise seemingly on the road to recovery, Kit partook of a late but hearty breakfast; then, as Papa was still sleeping, spent some time in the library with Squire Ashton, the reverend, the doctor and Hugo. He'd been hoping to engage the doctor in private further conversation regarding possible causes for Papa's indisposition, but instead found himself listening, with half an ear, while Hugo listed his own symptoms.

At first, Kit was inclined to dismiss Hugo's reported disorder as the sort of attention-seeking he most despised; but after surreptitiously examining him from over the top of his out-of-date newspaper, and noticing that actually a pallid-looking Hugo was being quite reticent about the cause of his ailment, he gave it rather more credence and listened intently. Squire Ashton also complained about feeling a trifle dyspeptic this morning, but Kit had the feeling that had more to do with the amount of alcohol he'd imbibed the previous evening than anything he had eaten.

'Nothing to do with the food,' volunteered Kit at this juncture. 'I ate well from every dish and I'm right as a trivet. No one else is ill as far as I'm aware. Just one of those things, Hugo. Take it easy today — you too, Squire. Sometimes your body requires a rest. Nothing to it.'

'Didn't know you'd studied medicine, dear boy,' said Doctor Bainbridge, in a mild tone belied by the gimlet gleam in his eyes.

After which Kit decided to excuse himself and seek out Georgie.

He knew he shouldn't, knew he should take this — whatever it was — very carefully indeed, but somehow he really wanted to be near her, really wanted to see her. Last night, when he'd suddenly come across her, clad in only a nightgown and shawl, standing in the shadows of the hallway, her eyes wide and troubled, her hair a fiery cloud round her shoulders, he'd wanted to put his arms around her, hold her close and tight. Only the concern for his Papa, and the ingrained knowledge of what was right and proper, had stopped him. One thing was clear to him: Georgie and her reputation were not to be compromised; and if that meant that he, Kit, had to rein in his instincts, ignore his every need and consider Georgie as Miss Rankin, teacher-cum-portrait-painter, and as such entitled to be treated with respect and courtesy, then so be it. But an awareness of all of that did not stop his impatience to see her this morning.

As he had expected, she was in the schoolroom studying her painting. His heart started to pound at the sight of her. To cover the sensation, he came up beside her and casually glanced at the sketch she was working from.

It was Lizzie. Pert and pretty, her expression showing an awareness that she was growing up and an impatience that it was not happening fast enough. Like himself, Lizzie would not have an easy adolescence.

Georgie put down her brush. 'Good morning,' she said guardedly.

'Good morning,' replied Kit. 'I hope

you slept well after your disturbed night.'

'Well enough. I'm glad to hear your Pa is recovering.'

Kit frowned. 'Yes . . . for now.'

'For now?'

His face broke into a smile he hoped was reassuring. 'Well, we are always concerned for his health . . . How did you get on with him yesterday, by the by?'

'Well, I think . . . I liked him, and I believe he quite liked me. I enjoyed drawing him. I'd like to paint him, but that would be too much to expect.'

'Would you object if I looked through your sketchbook?' He smiled. 'I promise I won't be too shocked by what I see.'

A delicate flush crept across her pale skin. 'I've learned to clothe my figure sketches now, even the preliminaries. After your reaction — well, I never wanted to see anyone so disgusted with me again. Pa was right: an artist sees things differently; but I didn't understand that then.'

Now he felt guilty. Guilty and apologetic. 'Neither did I. I'm sorry if I upset or frightened you.' He gave a laugh. 'To tell you the truth, I was upset and frightened myself.'

'Frightened? You? Of me?'

'I'd never met anyone like you. To think you were brave enough and talented enough to do what you did, because I knew it couldn't have been the first time you'd been out in those clothes, helped your father in the way that you did . . . Yes, I was frightened because you made me think; admit that there was another world out there, where young girls had to do whatever necessary to earn their bread . . . I suppose it made me slightly ashamed that I took things so for granted . . . You gave me just the dressing-down I needed. You may be sure your message found its mark.'

Her cool grey eyes looked up from her work and assessed him. He'd seen those same cool eyes turn fiery with fury, widen with fear; he hoped one day to see them smoulder with passion. Silently, she handed him her sketch-book. He took the book and stood staring at her for a moment longer. There was no need for him to speak.

'Then you'll understand,' she said slowly, 'when I ask you please to leave me alone. Not to upset me unnecessar-ily with wild talk and promises. Or to seek me out in the way you are doing. I would not like to lose my respect for you, nor yours for me, for I do believe you have some.' She bit her lip and looked away. 'Please try to understand the position I find myself in . . . '

What was he to do? His instincts were all wrong. Good God, it was improper of him to even be here with her alone.

Sketchbook in his hand, he turned and sat at the table. 'There,' he said. 'There's a respectable distance between us now. I am taking an interest in your work; the opportunity of examining the sketch I commissioned you to make of Papa . . . ' He stopped at the page where his father's face looked up at him through hooded eyes whose defiance failed to mask the fear in their depths.

He gave an involuntary gasp. 'You are clever beyond words, Georgie — it's perfect.'

She seemed surprised. 'Do you really like it? It was very fast, very spontaneous, and I'm afraid he wasn't very good at keeping still, but I was hopeful I might have managed something of the man.'

Kit looked backwards and forwards between the sketch and Georgie's glowing face. 'Oh, you have, Georgie, you have.'

He continued to leaf through the pages recognising from time to time the separate features of his siblings' faces: a nose here, lips or an eyebrow there.

'And how are you finding the group portrait?' he asked, handing back the book so she might continue working. 'Is it a long and tedious task?'

Georgiana laughed. 'Not at all. It's a pleasure. The children are fresh and open, and Arabella is — well, she's beautiful.'

'Yes, she is.'

'I've never met anyone with such perfect features.'

'Perfect.'

'Exceptional bone structure.'

'Certainly exceptional!'

Georgiana gave a sigh. 'It will be a pleasure to paint her. Her cheekbones, her nose . . . '

'You like her nose?'

'Oh, I do. It's an aristocratic yet classical nose. Just the right length, delicately defined nostrils . . . Don't you agree?'

'Well, if you like that sort of thing — I mean, nose.'

Georgiana laughed. 'How can such perfection fail to please?'

'I prefer softer features. A nose not too unlike yours, for example.'

'Mine?' She stared at him in disbelief. 'But mine is a splodge of a nose.'

'Even so. I happen to like splodges.

They can be an indication of great, great . . . '

Georgie raised an eyebrow.

'Great character!'

'I see. The character of a splodge. Thank you.'

Kit remained seated at the ink-stained table. His legs were cramped and his shoulder was playing him up despite, or maybe because of, its rapid healing. Even so, he was content to be sitting there watching, once again, Georgie's total absorption in her work.

A burning log shifted in the grate, sending out a shower of sparks. Glad of an excuse, Kit got to his feet and manoeuvred the log further back with the fire irons.

'Do you work for the whole morning without stopping?'

She glanced at him meaningfully. 'When I get the chance.' When he didn't smile, the glance became more penetrating, and she put down her brush and stood away from her easel. 'You appear distracted. You must be worried for your Pa?'

Kit gave a sigh. 'Is it that obvious? Yes, I was hoping to catch the doctor alone.' He grimaced. 'Not to be: Squire Ashton and Hugo are with him. Apparently Hugo is also ailing a little this morning . . . '

'And you think perhaps there was something wrong with the dishes served last night?'

Kit frowned as he sat down at the table again. 'No, I don't think that. I don't see how that's possible. Papa ate quite well, but not lavishly. There were no dishes that only he and Hugo ate; and from what Hugo said, although he was a little bilious, it had nowhere near the violence of Papa's attack — which, last night at least, the doctor found worrying to the extent of him suspecting . . . Well, no . . . Nothing, really.'

Georgie's gaze intensified further. 'What are you saying — exactly?'

'It sounds too melodramatic. But Bainbridge is a man of good sense and much experience. For him to mention poison . . . '

There was a sharp intake of breath. 'Poison?'

'I know — it's quite mad, is it not?'

'Why? How? And to put it in food . . . ' Disbelievingly, she shook her head. 'We all might have been ill . . . Surely too risky by far . . . But for a doctor to mention poison? He must have reason to believe it possible . . . Perhaps whoever did it meant it as a joke and didn't realise the implications?'

Kit straightened and eased his shoulder. 'Even Josh wouldn't do that. And with what? He has no access to poison. I'm willing to wager he went nowhere near the gardener's arsenic, he wouldn't even think of it.'

'Arsenic? The doctor thinks it was arsenic?'

'He doesn't know. Only that the sickness was so very extreme, it was likely to be something pretty lethal. We couldn't think of anything else.'

Georgiana turned a greenish white and sat down rather suddenly. 'Flake white,' she said. 'Flake white is very poisonous, it's made with lead. I don't use it until I have to, but it's better for flesh tones than anything. I keep it with the other toxic pigments on the very top shelf in a box with a lock.'

Her eyes strayed up to the top shelf, and Kit, following her gaze, was relieved to see a sturdy wooden box sitting in place next to a box of jigsaws that were too easy even for Josh now. They looked back at each other. Her eyes were wide and serious. For a long moment they stared at one another across the table. Then Kit gave a short laugh. 'Well, if it *was* that, Papa could never have reached it, even if he had the key.'

Georgie's eyes widened. 'You — you think your Pa might have taken it *deliberately*?'

'No! Never . . . ' He looked away and sighed. 'Truth is, I'm sure not . . . and yet — Bainbridge was worried about his state of mind, he told me as much before all this sickness business.'

'That's a nonsensical notion . . . It might have been so before now, I daresay — but oh, Kit, think! You'd just returned home. Your Papa was so very proud of you, so excited that you would be staying and helping with the estate. No, I won't believe it, not for a minute.'

Without any true enthusiasm, Kit nodded then glanced up at the top schoolroom shelf again. 'Perhaps we should check. Where do you keep the key?'

'Yes, of course . . . I keep it in the pocket of my smock.' She stood up and put her hand in the pocket. It was deep and contained small pieces of natural sponge, some charcoal, and a couple of paint-stained rags. She tumbled all of these onto the table. 'Funnily enough, today I was going to add flake white to my palette for the girls' dresses, which I hoped to make a start on this morning . . . ' Suddenly her face took on a worried expression as her fingers reached further. 'That's strange, I had it yesterday, but I can't find it . . . '

Immediately Kit was on his feet and dragging a chair across to the shelf.

'Don't you dare to get up there, Kit! If you fall on your shoulder . . . ' Almost before she'd finished speaking, Kit found she had crossed the room and, with an immodest hoist of her skirts, climbed onto the chair and was handing the box down to him. 'Josh can't reach this, in case you were wondering, and he's never really expressed an interest in where my paints are kept.'

It soon became apparent that the box was still locked.

'I'll have to force it,' said Kit, picking up a fire iron.

'No need,' said Georgie, passing him a hairpin. 'If you wriggle it a bit before you push it right in, you'll hear a click.'

'You've done this before?'

'Well, yes, but no-one would know that. Nobody has ever broken into it before — only me. I have a spare key in

London, it's not the first time I've lost one.'

Kit wriggled the pin. No click. Impatiently, Georgie took it from him. Their fingers brushed and Kit felt the sudden need to sit down again.

'Got it!' Georgie opened the lid. The powdered pigments were wrapped in small thick paper bags. 'This is the flake white,' said Georgie, immediately picking out the bulkiest bag there. 'It's treble-wrapped and it's — oh no! There's definitely some missing since yesterday! At least two teaspoonfuls! Oh no!' She stared uncomprehendingly at Kit. 'Who would do such a terrible thing?'

A sick feeling in his stomach, Kit stared back.

'This is my fault,' said Georgie. 'Pa always insisted to use extreme caution with flake white; it's the most poisonous of all the pigments. He insisted it was to be kept well away from children on as high a shelf as possible. I work from dark to light — use quite a lot of white, but not until I need to. Final flesh tones and highlights — sometimes for mixing. This morning was to have been the first time I've used it here . . . '

'So we don't know when it went missing? It could have been any time since you arrived.'

Miserably, Georgie nodded.

'There's nothing else for it,' said Kit eventually. 'I'll have to tell Bainbridge.'

★ ★ ★

Hardly able to believe that somehow she had been instrumental in the poisoning of dear Mr Merryfield, whom she found had come to mean a lot to her even though their acquaintance had been so brief, Georgiana stared wordlessly at Kit.

'I'll have to, don't you agree?'

'No, wait,' she said. 'Your father is safe for the moment. He's in his room with his valet and a footman, and very probably your stepmother. Surely nothing will befall him while we discuss this matter further? Let's not rush and spread panic unnecessarily.'

'There'll be no panic. Doctor Bainbridge must have been fairly sure to have suggested poison, so it will be no surprise to him. Then together we must work out why and who. Why anyone should want to, and who had the opportunity.'

'And who had anything to gain.'

As soon as she had framed the question, Georgie saw the obvious answer staring out of Kit's eyes as the realisation hit him. 'Well, *I* am the obvious choice,' he said.

'Don't be ridiculous!'

'I had the opportunity and the means. I had a drink with him in the library after dinner last evening, and could have easily slipped something in his glass ... God knows I've been hanging around the schoolroom for the last two days and could have helped myself to the lead white or whatever it's called, *and* I'm the direct heir to my father's estate

. . . I'd call that pretty damning!'

'Yes, but Kit, be sensible. We know it's not you, so who else could it be? Your stepmother hardly stands to gain — she would be displaced by your inheritance and lose any influence she now has over how things are run. Hugo's position would hardly change whether or not your Papa is alive. The doctor and his wife are surely above suspicion; and while I don't exactly like him, I can see no reason for Squire Ashton to be guilty.' She bit her lip as another thought occurred to her. Unwelcome as it was, she felt duty-bound to mention it.

'I suppose,' she went on in a small voice, 'I suppose *I* could be considered a suspect.'

Kit gave a twisted smile. 'Now who's being ridiculous?'

'If it *was* my paint — and it's looking very much as though it was — then I have permanent access to it.'

Kit raised an eyebrow. 'And motive?'

'Um, well, I hadn't got as far as that

yet, but I'm sure there must be one.'

'So we're left with Reverend Richardson, who I've known all my life and would suffer a troubled conscience over swatting a fly.'

By this time Georgiana was feeling the flutterings of fear under her ribcage. 'But I'm the unknown,' she said. 'I'm bound to be suspect . . . Let me think, just let me think . . . '

'Well, don't think too long,' said Kit. 'I'm feeling decidedly nervous about this whole thing, and would very much like to take Doctor Bainbridge into our confidence.'

At least he'd said 'our', as though they were working together on this.

'Supposing they say . . . ' said Georgie, hating every moment of this. 'Supposing they say I was setting my cap at you. That your father disapproved, but I was determined to have you, so I used the only means I had at my disposal and put flake white in one of his drinks! I was talking to him before dinner and he had a drink on the table right next to me.'

'What?' Kit was looking at her in horrified amusement. 'But who on earth is going to think that? That's outside of fantastical. Of course you wouldn't do that. It's been completely the other way around. *I've* been the one to do the pursuing.'

Georgie looked at him steadily. 'You think everyone will believe that? Face facts, Kit. I'm an impoverished teacher with everything to gain from ensnaring a rich husband. There are plenty who would use this position to entrap a good-looking, highly personable young man into marriage'

Kit gave a sudden grin. 'So, you think I'm good-looking and highly personable, do you?'

She couldn't stop herself. She smiled back. 'Not good-looking beyond the commonplace; but yes, on a good day, when the light's right — you pass muster.'

Kit laughed shortly, then became more serious. 'Nobody's going to honestly believe you suddenly decide to poison Papa in order to trap me into marriage.'

'They might,' repeated Georgie stubbornly. 'Who else would even know that flake white is so deadly? You certainly didn't! I did warn the children not to touch the box, though. I believe I might have mentioned that many paint pigments are toxic in front of Arabella; and of course, Hugo is interested in painting, although I rather thought not quite as interested as he pretended.'

Kit lifted an ironic eyebrow. 'No, he was a deal more interested in the painter, was he not?'

Georgie shrugged. 'Oh, I've met Hugo's sort before, and am well able to deal with him.'

Kit frowned. 'So, Arabella? No, I can't think she would do my father any harm, and I'm sure anyway she'd do nothing to hasten my inheriting Markington. I'd have far too much power for her liking, and if she argued with me she knows I'd have no compunction in banishing her to the dower house.' He smiled. 'She'd . . . ' He broke off mid-sentence as though an unwelcome thought had suddenly struck him.

'What? You've thought of something?' Kit gave a sharp intake of breath. 'No, not really. No, not at all.'

But, Georgie thought, he'd definitely hesitated. There was something he didn't want to share with her. 'Well, if not Arabella, who and why? As I said before, I'm the unknown quantity; I'm bound to be the suspect.'

Kit's eyes went back to the wooden box. 'Who else had access to the key?'

'To my smock? Well, the children, I suppose, here in the schoolroom; and the housemaid, when it was left in my room.'

'Did you ever leave it unattended here?'

'No I don't think so . . . ' Suddenly she remembered hurrying to lunch in order not to keep Arabella waiting. 'No, wait a minute . . . Yes, I left it here draped over the chair, but you were with me then, don't you remember? When we went off to take luncheon yesterday?'

'I didn't notice your smock. I noticed your eyes. I noticed the paint on your nose and wondered if I dared to wipe it off. I noticed your smile . . . '

'Stop it. This is serious!'

Something of her fear must have been in her voice, because Kit moved as though to reassure her, maybe put an arm round her shoulder — but then, as though with an effort, stopped himself. 'You're right. It is serious. We have to go to Bainbridge. We have no choice . . . How much of that paint would kill someone?'

'I have no idea. For heaven's sake, Kit! I don't go around poisoning people . . . I was always told never to inhale it, even the smallest amount could be lethal — but that was Pa speaking, and he wanted to keep me safe.'

'Of course.' He looked back at the small bag containing the flake white. 'Two teaspoonfuls missing? All of it might not have been used yet. Which means . . . '

Georgie felt a shudder go through her. 'Which means, that the killer still has it!'

10

'So now you know as much as we do.'

After Kit stopped speaking, the silence in the room was thick with unasked questions.

Arabella, Doctor Bainbridge, the Reverend Richardson, Hugo and Georgiana were gathered together in the small drawing room. Outside, a watery sun was attempting an appearance. Georgie noticed a shaft of it, low in the sky, cutting through the window, lighting a crystal vase with a rainbow of colours.

Doctor Bainbridge looked grim but calm. It had been at his suggestion that they all meet here, and that together he, Kit and Georgiana would tell them of the missing pigment. No reason, he'd said, to alarm the entire household. Of necessity Joshua's valet, a devoted family servant of years' standing and above reproach, had been given the basic facts and told to keep a tight watch over his master, but so far no one else had been informed.

'My God.' Arabella, the first to speak, turned an accusing stare in Georgie's direction. 'How has this happened? Miss Rankin, what have you to say?'

Even though she had been expecting this, Georgiana winced. 'Very little, Mrs Merryfield. I am as baffled as anyone. I've always kept my pigments under lock and key . . . Nonetheless, I have to take some responsibility . . . I thought it was safe in a locked box on a high shelf, but it wasn't.'

Arabella's cold gaze swept over her. 'Indeed.'

'More to the point,' said Kit, 'who stole it and administered it, and why?'

Hugo was still a sickly white and the Reverend Richardson's mouth had rounded in amazement.

'M-maybe one of the children?' queried Hugo.

'Never,' said Arabella.

'As a joke, perhaps?' Hugo quavered bravely on.

'As a *joke*?' thundered Arabella.

'Josh is nowhere near tall enough to reach the shelf, and anyway he's too taken up with the new puppies and the snow to get up to much mischief,' said Kit.

'Out of the question,' Arabella agreed emphatically. 'And how was it administered? Joshua was well at dinner — weary, but otherwise in robust health when he retired. So when and how did he take the poison?'

Doctor Bainbridge cleared his throat. 'We think perhaps in his indigestion medicine glass. It's always kept on his bedside table, and the medicine is white in colour. If it contained white liquid, anyone would assume it was the medicine. And it's taken as and when required . . . Unfortunately, the glass has since been washed, and the valet can't remember with any certainty if the glass was empty or not when he left Mr Merryfield last evening.'

'So anyone could have put it in there at any time,' said Hugo. 'Surely, then, it must have been one of the servants?'

'Why would they?' asked Kit.

Hugo licked dry lips. 'Well, your father could be difficult. His disability, you know . . . '

'I don't doubt it. But they understood. You know that, Hugo, you must do. They love him . . . ' His voice shook a little. 'Damn it — we all do! Surely no one would do this! It beggars belief!'

The reverend shook his head. 'It has been known,' he started, 'that when invalids lose their faith, they might be tempted to put an end . . . '

'No!' said Arabella, Kit and Georgie, forcefully and in unison.

Georgie felt Arabella's eyes upon her. 'Miss Rankin, you have an opinion on this?'

Georgiana blanched. 'Only that I spent some time yesterday executing a pencil drawing of Mr Merryfield. During the short time I was with him, he struck me as looking forward to the

291

future, to spending time with his family. He spoke of you all in such glowing terms . . . No, I cannot think he was planning to take poison — and anyhow, he couldn't have reached it, could he?'

There was the rasping sound of Doctor Bainbridge's throat being cleared. 'The only thing I know for sure about lead poisoning — and I believe flake white is made from lead carbonate — is that it's a cumulative poison. Miss Rankin tells us she has two teaspoons of the stuff missing. In my opinion, only a very little of that was used, but caused such a violent reaction that it has almost certainly been, in the main, expelled from the body.'

'What does that prove?' asked Hugo.

'Well, nothing really, other than that whoever took the poison still has some in reserve. Perhaps the plan was to use it slowly, a day at a time — a gradual process, if you like. Foul play would never be suspected.'

'But why?' It was Kit who asked the

question they were all thinking. 'This is dangerous,' he went on. 'We have to ask the children, we have to warn them. There is nothing else for it. I know, ma'am, I know it goes against the grain — but suppose they come across the cached poison accidentally? Suppose it has been hidden, and they find it and handle it incorrectly. Put their fingers to their mouths? The consequences could be dire . . . The whole household will have to be told. Nothing else for it.'

There was a long-drawn-out sigh and, white-faced, Arabella sat down. 'Much more of this and I shall have hysterics.'

'No you won't,' said Kit firmly. 'You're made of sterner stuff. It's your job to keep calm and preserve practicality.'

Georgiana gave a weak smile. 'What would you like me to do, Mrs Merryfield? Shall I fetch the children and Miss Garvie?'

'Perhaps you should ask Kit, since he seems to be in charge.' Arabella's voice had taken on an edge of asperity. Then she motioned with her hand. 'Yes, of course, thank you. Forgive me. This has all been rather a shock. I'll call Brewer and ask him to summon the above-stairs staff. Hugo, perhaps you would be good enough to ask Squire and Mrs Ashton and Mrs Bainbridge to come too . . . And of course, you're right, Kit, and thank God you're here.'

Georgie didn't wait to hear any more. She fetched her cloak and prepared to go out into the cold in her hastily-fastened boots.

Thankfully she didn't have far to go. She met Lizzie first who was already on her way to the house, the rest of the bedraggled group following behind her, their eyes sparkling, their cheeks flushed from the cold, and every one of them smiling.

'We've had such larks,' said Josh. 'I fell off and nearly buried Lizzie, and she chased me and put snow down my back. Then Jane and Charles went the wrong way down the dipping and ended up in the ditch, and Charles had to carry Jane out but we're not to tell Mama that bit. I don't see why he had to carry her anyway, she's quite capable of walking, but that's girls for you . . . '

Quickly, Georgie explained that they were all to present themselves in the small drawing room, quick as you like, just to tidy themselves a little, if they pleased. She assured Jane that yes, Papa was indeed in good health; and no, she couldn't tell them what it was all about, only to hurry please because it was quite important.

She watched as the children went in to change their boots, then set about finding Miss Garvie.

Somehow, within twenty minutes or so, the drawing room was full to bursting, with more staff than Georgie had realised existed, and the family and guests.

Having found Miss Garvie in her room, sewing a sampler or some such thing, it seemed wisest to stay close to her just inside the door; and although she was desperate to be near Kit, for reassurance and comfort, she only shot him a slight smile across the room.

Doctor Bainbridge stood up.

From the corner of her eye, Georgie saw the door behind her edge open and Hugo sidle in.

The doctor was brief and to the point. 'Some very poisonous substance has gone missing,' he started. 'We all need to be vigilant, because it is extremely dangerous even in small quantities.'

There was a lot of shuffling amongst the staff. Miss Garvie gave a small squeak, then covered her mouth with her hand. But nobody stepped forward or said anything. Doctor Bainbridge went on to describe that it was a white powder, innocuous in appearance, but that its effects could be lethal.

Georgie searched round for the children — eventually, through a convenient gap between various domestics, catching a glimpse of Josh, whose eyes looked ready to pop from his head.

Arabella rose to her feet, asked for everyone's co-operation, and please, if anyone had any ideas as to what had happened to the substance, to speak up — or, if they were too shy, to report to their senior as soon as possible. 'I cannot emphasize enough,' she finished, 'how very important this is. Thank you all for your attention.'

With more shuffling and some nervous murmurings, the above-stairs staff filed from the room. Soon, apart from Brewer and one footman, there were only the main family and guests left.

'Coffee, ma'am?' suggested Brewer.

'That would be timely,' answered Arabella.

As the footman left the room, Georgie resolved not to take sugar — just in case.

★   ★   ★

'I can't believe,' said Kit, after a pause that seemed to him to have gone on far too long, 'that one of the servants is responsible for this.'

'Well, what's the alternative?' asked Squire Ashton, whose colour was high with excited animation.

Kit swallowed. What indeed? That it was one of the people left in the room now? The good doctor and his wife? Unthinkable! The Reverend Richardson? Laughable! Cousin Hugo? No good reason. And Squire Ashton? He had no motive that Kit could imagine.

That left, Miss Garvie. Miss Garvie, who needed smelling salts at the smallest sign of unrest; who fluttered and fussed her way through life but whose only wish was to fade into the wallpaper.

He frowned because of course, there was one other.

His stepmother was still very pale. She sat upright, one hand on the armrest of her chair; but, Kit observed, the other in her lap was constantly pleating and re-pleating the fabric of her gown. She glanced across at Hugo.

Only a fleeting glance, but Kit noticed it. Arabella was nervous. Arabella had undoubtedly been having a fling with Hugo, but it was difficult to imagine what she would gain by her husband's death. Kit knew her well enough to realise she wouldn't take kindly to be shunted off to the dower house, even if it meant that she could carry on her affair with Hugo . . . but, discerning again the violet stains beneath her eyes and remembering her concern for his father the night before, he couldn't believe her capable of such treachery.

Finally his eyes turned towards Georgie.

'Yes,' said Squire Ashton, following his gaze. 'The newcomer. How much do you know about this Miss Rankin?'

'Indeed,' Hugo agreed quickly. 'After all, she's the owner of the pigment. She's the only one who knew how lethal it was.'

Georgiana bristled with indignation.

'Why, in that case, would I even mention it? I'd have been wiser to let everyone think Mr Merryfield had suffered food poisoning, wouldn't I? Anyway, Hugo, earlier you took a great deal of interest in my paints, telling me how proficient you were in their use!'

'You say that now,' accused Hugo. 'It's only your word against mine.'

'Yes, why should we believe her?' asked Squire Ashton, his little squinty eyes crinkling with triumph. 'I happen to know she's a compulsive liar. She used to dress in boy's clothes and go with her father to paint portraits of men. How duplicitous and disgusting was that?'

There was a gasp all around, the loudest emanating from Miss Garvie.

With extreme difficulty, Kit restrained himself from punching Squire Ashton and telling Miss Garvie to control herself and her gasping with shock at every opportunity. Somehow, he contained himself. Georgie's face was flaming: whether with embarrassment or fury, he was unsure.

'Be very careful who you slander. Miss Rankin is just as much my father's guest as you are,' he started.

'They're in it together,' interrupted Hugo.

'What on earth are you talking about?' Arabella's voice cut in.

'I heard Kit and his father arguing. In the study after dinner last evening.'

'What about?'

'It's my belief Kit's sweet on Miss Rankin. Mr Merryfield forbade the friendship and threatened to send her packing. That must have been it,' went on Hugo, warming to his theme. 'They must have hatched the plot together!'

Kit laughed. 'Really? Have you taken leave of your senses. Hugo? Do you not realise how ridiculous you sound?'

'Yes,' agreed Arabella. 'You do indeed make yourself ridiculous. Hugo . . . ' She looked over to where the children were grouped. 'Children, disregard what you've heard.' She stopped suddenly. 'Where's Lizzie?' she asked Miss Garvie.

Miss Garvie appeared not to hear. 'What a very distressing scene . . . '

'Yes. Where *is* Lizzie?' repeated Georgie.

'Well, I don't know why you're asking me,' said Miss Garvie, huffily patting her hair.

Georgie gave a sharp intake of breath, then exhaled again because, as though on cue, Lizzie slipped into the room.

'What's happened then?' asked Lizzie, squeezing next to Josh on a chair made for one. 'Why is everyone looking so solemn?'

'Because we're talking about poison, silly!' said Josh. 'One tiny bit could kill you stone dead.' He bulged his eyes and made gagging noises, put a hand to his throat and slumped against the chair back.

'It's not funny, Josh,' said Arabella.

As if suddenly sensing the tension in the room, Lizzie stared around.

'I've missed something. What were all the servants doing here? Will someone please tell me what's going on?'

Jane turned to look at her sister.

'Miss Rankin told us we were to come here right away. Where were you?'

Lizzie went pink. 'I don't see why I have to say . . . I was just tidying myself like Mama always tells us to before we present ourselves in the drawing room. Don't you, Mama?'

'You were in the water closet, weren't you?' said Josh

'Well, what if I was? I had to go and I had to tidy myself. Not like you; you're filthy and your hair's all sticking up,' replied Lizzie hotly.

There was a tap on the door and Brewer, followed by a footman, entered with a tray of coffee.

Arabella put a wan hand to her head. 'Children, children! That's enough squabbling. Please, someone explain to Lizzie . . . Yes, thank you, Brewer. Serve it straight away if you please.'

Kit stepped forward. 'Lizzie, something very disturbing has happened. Some of Miss Rankin's paint has gone missing. It's white powder in a small white paper bag, and it's extremely poisonous. If you know where it is or indeed anything about it, please tell us.'

A sly look came over Lizzie's face. 'That's easy.'

For a moment, Kit was baffled. Then he smiled. 'Lizzie, this isn't the time for attention-seeking.'

'It's easy,' she said with a toss of her head. 'I bet it's in the candle box in Papa's study!'

Kit sat down rather suddenly. Papa must have attempted suicide after all.

'No,' he said aloud, every instinct he possessed telling him this could not be the case.

Despite the shock in Arabella's eyes, she seemed to recover first. 'Brewer,' she said. 'Leave the coffee. Go and see if what Miss Lizzie says is correct. Take someone with you.'

Brewer, who had frozen with the coffee pot in mid-air, now replaced it carefully on the tray. 'Certainly, ma'am. Come, Frimble!' He motioned to the footman.

After they'd left, Georgie asked

quietly, 'Lizzie what made you look in the candle box?'

Lizzie squirmed. 'I know I'm not allowed in the study — in the normal way of things, no one is — but Papa doesn't mind because I cheer him up, he says, so I often go. Sometimes he gives me one of his indigestion mints.'

'When did you find the pois- . . . the white powder?' Kit asked

'Just now, that's why I was late. Oh, I wasn't looking for it,' said Lizzie. 'I was watching the person who put it in there.'

Every eye in the room was on Lizzie. She sat back, enjoying the attention.

'Who?' asked Arabella in a cracked voice. 'Who was it, Lizzie? This isn't a game, it's very important.'

Lizzie's face crumpled. 'You won't like it, Mama. You won't like it if I say, I know you won't!'

'She doesn't know,' scoffed Josh. 'You know what she's like. Always creeping round spying on people and making things up.'

'I do know,' screamed Lizzie. 'I do. I do. It was him!'

At the same time as Brewer came into the room, bearing the wooden candle box in one hand and a small paper bag of white powder in the other, Hugo leapt from his chair.

'I can explain,' he said. 'I can explain everything.'

Arabella's face twisted. 'Oh, dear God! Not now, Hugo! Miss Rankin, please establish if this is indeed your pigment and the amount you're missing . . . Thank you. Brewer. Please finish serving the coffee to our guests, then inform the servants *only* that the powder is found. Hugo, I suggest that you accompany Kit and me to the study, and we'll discuss this in private . . . I apologise to you all for this most distressing . . . ' As her words ran out, she waved a tired hand in the air.

Kit felt sick. Sick and disappointed. He tried to make no judgement. He had to at least listen, he told himself, as he followed Hugo and Arabella to the forbidden territory of Papa's study.

After motioning to Hugo and Kit to sit down, Arabella sat herself behind Papa's desk.

Hugo remained silent, his eyes downcast, and Arabella looked too exhausted to speak

'I think I know what happened,' said Kit eventually. 'You heard Papa and me talking last evening, didn't you, Hugo? That part at least is true. To be brief, Papa wanted Hugo to leave, or at least be housed in separate premises on the estate. My homecoming seemed a good opportunity to do that.' He paused. 'I believe we know the reasoning behind his thinking.'

'Dear God! You mean he knew?' Arabella put a hand to her brow.

'Ma'am, I've been here only a few days, and I knew . . . However, at the time, I felt it my business to remonstrate with Papa. I pointed out that Hugo had worked hard for the estate . . . '

'I had,' said Hugo looking up at last.

307

'Very hard. I've made no end of improvements.'

'Quite . . . And you could see it all going for nothing, couldn't you? All that work, all that careful manipulating in order to prove yourself indispensable. Spoilt at a stroke, all because I had turned up and intended to stay? I'm sorry, Hugo, I suppose I should have been more tactful. I thought I had time to make a friend of you.'

Hugo looked at him with loathing. 'Friend! You jest! I could see how it would be. Everyone simpering round you . . . I'd be pushed into a backwater in no time. My life would be nothing to how I'd planned it.'

'And just how was that, Hugo? Let me guess. Maybe I would have died out in the Peninsula? Thousands did. That would have been convenient, wouldn't it? And maybe Papa would soon die too, whether of a broken heart or a fall or something else that would have been difficult to prove; and maybe good old reliable Hugo, who'd done such a sterling job in the past, would have consoled the grieving widow, risen to a position of power, and taken care of all estate matters until Josh came of age, eh? How does that sound?'

'You're guessing! You have no proof.'

'Not a jot,' said Kit. 'Only a bag of white pigment and a child's story that she saw you hide it earlier.'

'She probably took it herself, intending some mischief. It's true what Josh says — she's always spying on people and causing trouble!'

'That's enough, Hugo!' Shakily, Arabella stood up.

'I'd like you to go now, please. I don't want to see your face again until our guests have left and we can decide what to do about this unholy mess. I'll arrange for your meals to be sent up on a tray . . . No, I'm not about to argue the point!'

For a long moment after a tight-faced Hugo had left the room, Arabella stood staring at Kit. 'What a mess I've made of everything,' she said. 'You must hate me more than ever now.'

'On the contrary,' said Kit surprising even himself, 'I am starting to learn to quite like you.'

★ ★ ★

Somehow, the day went on.

By tacit consent, Miss Garvie and Georgie colluded in occupying the children until schoolroom luncheon, sticking to the story that the pigment had been found by Hugo, put into the candle box for safekeeping, and no harm done; and that Squire Ashton had made a genuine mistake in thinking Georgie's poor dead brother Tommy was actually Georgie.

'*As if!*' said Josh witheringly. 'Anyone can see Miss Rankin's a girl!'

Georgie never knew how the adults explained the situation to one another, but found that when she was noticed, she was treated with respect. In the main, she stayed out of sight and planned to work on her canvas the entire afternoon.

She tried hard not to think about Kit.

Miss Garvie confided that she'd heard, through the servants' grapevine, that it was deemed wise, now that the roads were passable, that the Ashtons should cut short their visit by a day and leave as early as possible the next morning.

Nothing was seen of Hugo, and Arabella spent most of her time with her husband, who she said hoped to be well enough to attend meals the next day.

Lizzie told her story several times over to anyone who would listen. How she had of necessity visited the downstairs water closet first, then was on the way to tidying herself when she saw Hugo go into Papa's study. 'He just didn't look right,' she said. 'And *no-one's* allowed without invitation, and I knew Papa was still in bed, so I watched round the side of the door. He took the little bag out of his pocket and put it under the candles. I thought it was strange, but I knew I was late, and had to change my skirt because it was wet with snow . . . So that's what I did. Then, when I came back to the drawing room, I saw all the servants coming out and I knew something funny had been going on . . . '

Georgiana heaved a sigh of relief and got back to work in the schoolroom. Miss Garvie came in and watched her for a while, sitting quietly and occasionally making up the fire as unobtrusively as possible, as though the sound of a poker in the grate would disturb Georgie's concentration and ruin the portrait.

Poor, timid Miss Garvie, Georgiana wondered if a similar future waited for her, and gave an involuntary shiver. Then she set her shoulders back, because all too soon she would be on her way back to London and her work as a teacher of young ladies in the art of watercolour painting.

Soon Miss Garvie became bored and went off to see the housekeeper, with whom she'd promised to share a cup of tea and a chat. Georgie guessed that the chat might include the strange events of the morning being discussed at length, and with many different surmises as to what it was really all about.

The painting was coming on quite well. The tonal values were making themselves felt now, and it was time to take a break. She stepped back from her easel and stretched, then turned at the sound of steps outside in the corridor. Her heart started to beat a little faster, but it was only a footman bearing a tray of tea and sandwiches. Dear Miss Garvie, she must have thought to have some refreshment sent.

The footman placed the tray on the table. It was only when he'd gone that she noticed there were two cups and saucers next to the teapot. Miss Garvie's instructions must have been misunderstood.

'Ah, tea's arrived. Good!'

It was Kit.

Her mouth went dry.

'Well, say you're pleased to see me. Don't I even get a smile?'

Georgie grinned obligingly. 'I apologise.'

'We can be as cosy as you like,' said Kit his eyes crinkling at the corners. 'We won't be interrupted, and before you start to fuss and say it's improper, Papa knows, Arabella knows, and everyone is happy.'

'Arabella?'

'The Langley connection made a difference.'

'I'm estranged from the Langleys.'

'Even so.'

'And — knows what, exactly?'

'Knows that I am here with you now — having tea and a *private* conversation — at last!'

Georgie sat down, mainly because her knees seemed to have turned to jelly. 'Well, what are we to talk about?'

He didn't answer immediately. Instead, he took a chair opposite and started to pour the tea. When he looked up, Georgie was surprised to see that he looked shy. 'About that . . . I've suddenly some-how managed to fall ridiculously in love with you . . . Er, would you like one lump or two?'

'Um. None, no sugar for me. And you're right. It is ridiculous. We've hardly known each other more than three days.'

'That's the ridiculous part. I feel I've known you all of my life, but I understand if you don't feel the same way, and I'm sorry if I rushed my fences and frightened you, didn't show you the respect you deserved. But Papa's right, sometimes it happens like that.'

'You'd soon get tired of me if you got to know me better.'

'No, I wouldn't. I'd never get tired of you. I'd never get tired of watching the way your eyes change from one mood to another, the way your hair curls at your neck. The way you stand so straight, and your lips twitch when you find something amusing . . . The way when I kissed you, you wanted to kiss me back, then wished you hadn't.'

'B-but I'm just an art teacher.'

'Just a? *Just* a? You're very talented, but I wouldn't care even if you weren't ... I agree, we need some time — we both do — to get used to the situation and all its complications. All I'm asking is for you to give me that time. For you to know that my intentions are honourable, and that — I love you.'

He loved her.

'You love me?' The words trembled on her lips.

'I do, but the question is ... '

'Yes,' said Georgie, smiling — a real smile this time. 'Yes, I do, I do, I do!'

Kit sprang to his feet. 'You do?'

'Always,' she said simply. 'Ever since I first met you.'

He came round the table and, holding both her hands, drew her to her feet. 'Georgie ... '

She never heard what he intended to say, because when he opened his lips they came firmly down on hers, and after that she just stopped hearing anything. Just gave in to the most wonderful sensation she'd felt in her life.

He loved her, she loved him.

It was simple, really.

We do hope that you have enjoyed reading this large print book.

Did you know that all of our titles are available for purchase?

We publish a wide range of high quality large print books including:
Romances, Mysteries, Classics
General Fiction
Non Fiction and Westerns

Special interest titles available in large print are:
The Little Oxford Dictionary
Music Book, Song Book
Hymn Book, Service Book

Also available from us courtesy of Oxford University Press:
Young Readers' Dictionary
(large print edition)
Young Readers' Thesaurus
(large print edition)

For further information or a free brochure, please contact us at:
Ulverscroft Large Print Books Ltd.,
The Green, Bradgate Road, Anstey,
Leicester, LE7 7FU, England.
Tel: (00 44) **0116 236 4325**
Fax: (00 44) **0116 234 0205**

Other titles in the
Linford Romance Library:

CHRISTMAS AT CASTLE ELRICK

Fenella J. Miller

Severely injured in the Napoleonic Wars, Sir Ralph Elrick has been brooding in his castle for years, waiting for Miss Verity Sanderson to reach her majority and marry him. The week before Christmas, she sets off to his ancestral home to become his wife. But Castle Elrick is a cold, unwelcoming place — and Ralph and his small staff are not the only residents. Will Christmas be a joyous celebration, or will the ghosts of Castle Elrick force the newlyweds apart?

THE ROSE AND THE REBEL

Valerie Holmes

In stifling summer heat, Miss Penelope Rose decides to take a swim — scandalously, in an outdoor pool on her father's estate. Having sent off her maid, Penelope strips to her underclothes and indulges herself in the coolness of the secluded water. But when she climbs out, wearing only her soaked chemise, her dress has disappeared! To make matters considerably more embarrassing, she finds herself standing face to face with the culprit — Mr Lucas Bleakly, the eligible bachelor son of the local reverend . . .

AS THE FOUR WINDS BLOW

June Davies

Isobel Blundell isn't looking forward to her special birthday. Her archaeologist husband, Douglas, is in South America, and she and their three children miss him sorely. On her birthday, Isobel's mother Ailsa, and sisters Kirsty and Dorrie, give her Douglas's gift — an airline ticket! Overjoyed, Isobel sets off for a holiday with him at the dig. But heartache, danger, conflict and tragedy lie ahead for the whole family — those at home, as well as Isobel and Douglas in South America.

THE INHERITANCE

Wendy Kremer

Sara expects that when a local group of people from her village who want a say in the future of an empty manor house confront the new owners, her own loyalty will be clear and simple — but that's before she is unexpectedly chosen to talk things over with the new owner, Madame Jannet Rogard, and her attractive son, Nick, at their château in France. What's more, even though Sara and Nick come from different worlds, there's no denying the attraction growing between them . . .